Queenie's Castle

Queenie's Castle

LENA KENNEDY

BCA

LONDON NEW YORK SYDNEY TORONTO

This edition published 1993
by BCA by arrangement with
Little, Brown and Company

A CIP catalogue record for this book
is available from the British Library.

CN 1158

Typeset by Hewer Text Composition Services, Edinburgh
Printed in England by Clays Ltd, St Ives plc

Queenie's Castle

Chapter One

Mistaken Identity

Even for November, the night was cold. It was late and the whole of London was shrouded in smog – thick, choking smog, a real pea-souper. It brought a filthy yellow mist which crept up the nostrils and stung the eyes, choking throats and killing off the sick and vulnerable. People out in a night of smog, the population of the great city, would wrap scarves over their mouths in order to breathe, anxious to prevent the evil air creeping down into their lungs as they hurried home from their offices and factories to their warm household fires and hot food. It was impossible to see further than a few inches.

On this night, the buses had stopped. A long line of them was halted at the roadside. 'All change!' the conductor called to the last passenger – a man who had fallen asleep on the top deck.

The man awoke with a start. 'Where are we?' He peered out of the window but could see nothing.

'We are at Aldgate, sir,' the conductor replied. 'But we're not moving any more tonight. The fog is too thick.'

The passenger got up from his seat and stumbled down the stairs. 'What the devil do you mean?' he demanded. 'I was supposed to get off at Baker Street. How am I going to get back there?'

'Sorry, sir,' returned the conductor with a shrug, 'it's been a hazardous journey tonight and I'll be very pleased to pack up and go home.'

The passenger stood looking confused and then the bus driver joined them on the platform. An irate and tired little cockney, he was not so polite. 'Are you getting orf, mate? I'll tell yer, this bus ain't movin' no more tonight.'

'Damn and blast,' said the passenger. 'Where's the tube station?'

'It's that way,' said the conductor, pointing out into the thick yellow air.

'You won't arf be lucky,' cackled the driver. 'It's past midnight by now.'

The man jumped from the bus and stood for a moment on the pavement, as he tried to get his bearings. His shoulders drooped wearily and his short straggly beard was covered with drops of moisture from the thick fog. He was tall and thin with long limbs and sensitive long-fingered hands. His broad face was drawn and tired, the skin taut over his cheek bones. In one hand he carried a battered old leather briefcase. 'What a fool I am,' he muttered. 'How could I have slept through my bus stop? I must have been so tired. I shouldn't have stayed so long correcting those exercises. Damned illiterate hooligans! I don't know why I bother.'

Joe Walowski was a teacher at a sixth-form college in a run-down part of Paddington. Towards the end of term he often became so exhausted that he would drop off into a deep sleep as soon as he sat down. To relax meant to doze off. It was most annoying. And now he had the long dreary journey back to his lodgings ahead of him. What a miserable life!

Dejectedly, he pulled up his coat collar and set

off. Lost in his melancholic thoughts, he took little notice of his surroundings. People stumbled past, voices drifted through the yellow haze. It was like a lost world.

Suddenly a high-pitched note pierced the freezing air. It was the sound of a ship's siren. That must mean that he was near the river. Joe made his way towards the siren noise, but found himself up against a brick wall. 'Oh blast!' he exclaimed. Turning round in confusion, he did not know where to go.

It was then that the woman appeared, smiling at him like a phantom from the night. Overhead, the light from a yellow lamp tried valiantly to compete with the gloom. And there she was, sauntering slowly towards him, small and slim, wearing a short miniskirt, a tight blouse, and a black leather jacket.

To Joe, standing forlornly beside the brick wall, she was a warm and pleasant sight. As she came closer, he could smell the cheap perfume she wore. The mysterious effect was spoiled somewhat when she opened her rosy mouth. 'Christ!' she said, with a strong cockney accent. 'Ain't it foggy? I can't see a bleedin' thing.'

Joe was too surprised to answer. He simply stared straight at her, fixated by her violet eyes and the deep cleavage where her plump white breasts nestled in her blouse.

'Come on then,' she said, grabbing his arm. 'Let's go down the café, it's cold out here.'

Astounded, but more than willing, Joe went along with her. He was being picked up, and it was just as well, he thought, since this girl clearly knew the narrow back streets very well indeed.

They made their way through the fog and at last a glint of pale light crossed the path ahead. Squinting up, Joe could just make out the words: Fred's Café.

Inside the dingy room, there were a few marble-topped tables, a juke box and a one-armed bandit. They all seemed to crowd the grubby grey linoleum floor. At the far end, behind the cramped counter, and standing near a dirty steaming urn, was the proprietor, Fred. A big fat man, rat-faced, grimy and unshaven, he was slowly pouring boiling water from the urn into a blue enamel teapot.

'Thank Gawd!' exclaimed Joe's blonde companion. 'It ain't arf flamin' foggy out there.' She rubbed her hands together to restore the circulation in her fingers.

Feeling rather bewildered, Joe hesitated in the doorway.

'Come in, guv'nor!' called the woman. 'Put the wood in the 'ole!'

As Blondie was pointing at the door, Joe realised that he was supposed to shut it. This he did nervously as Blondie took his briefcase from him and placed it on top of the counter. 'We'll have a cuppa first. The boys'll be here soon and we can sort out the loot then.'

Joe did not understand what she was talking about but he was happy to be able to wrap his hands around the heavy mug of tea that was handed to him. As his hands warmed up, Joe sat blinking his eyes which were red and sore from the ravages of the smog. In confusion, he watched Blondie carefully and tried to follow what she was saying. He generally prided himself as someone who was good at languages. Being of Polish origin but brought up in New York City, he spoke several languages fluently. But this cockney accent at full speed was impossible to translate.

Blondie suddenly went off into a cascade of giggles which sounded like dirty water going down a drain. It was infectious. Joe found himself smiling as he sipped the steaming brown tea and watched her with amazement.

Blondie abruptly stopped laughing and reached into her jacket pocket. Her hand came out empty. 'Nuffink in here,' she said with a grimace. 'Got a tenner, mate?' she asked Joe. 'By the way, my name's Maisie.' She smiled sweetly at him.

Joe considered for a moment and then put his hand into his trouser pocket to produce two six-penny pieces. Maisie took them from him and put them straight into the juke box. She selected some music, and within seconds the café was filled with the stereophonic sound of pop music. Maisie began clicking her fingers and dancing in time to the music. She cavorted about the small floor space, with her arms waving and her hips swinging.

Joe closed his eyes wearily and sighed. He loathed pop music. This racket was the last thing he needed. He opened his eyes slowly and stared with puzzlement at Maisie. She was still bopping to the music but had sidled up to the counter. She glanced surreptitiously at Joe, who pretended to have his eyes closed still, then she leaned over the counter and produced another briefcase which looked identical to his. What was she doing? Joe rubbed his eyes and looked again. There was one case on the counter. Had he imagined that there were two or not? Was he suffering from double vision in his exhaustion? The sooner he got home to bed, the better. The music was awful, and made his head throb. Then at last it was over, the money in the juke box had run out. Now Maisie was at the door arguing with someone. Joe turned to see a thin-faced youth wearing a black leather jacket decorated with what looked like a swastika. In his hand he swung a crash helmet.

Maisie was quite agitated. 'Where have you been,

Nosher?' she demanded. 'Supposed to look after me, wasn't yer?'

'I got lost in the fog, Maisie,' Nosher whined. 'Let me just sit down and have a cheese sandwich,' he said. 'I'm starvin'.'

'That's it, all yer fink about is eating,' Maisie declared belligerently. 'I done the job all on me own, and where was you?' she yelled.

Nosher lowered his voice. 'Where is he?' he asked.

'Over there.' Maisie jerked a thumb in Joe's direction.

Joe listened to this exchange and wondered what it was all about. But he was too tired to care. He gazed out of the grimy window and was relieved to see that the smog was clearing a little. The shadows were becoming a pearly grey and the yellow clouds were dispersing as the rain won its battle with the fog.

By now Maisie and her friend had left the café and crossed the road to the telephone box. Peering through the window, Joe could just see Maisie's golden hair as she and Nosher both squeezed into the red kiosk. From their gestures, the two of them seemed to be quarrelling.

Joe had had enough of the night's events. It was time to part company with new acquaintances. He picked up his briefcase, nodded to Fred, who was wiping the tables, and slipped out into the street.

As Joe Walowski headed home, a lively scene was being enacted in Fred's Café. A few minutes after Joe had left, another young man arrived. He was huge, broad-set and smartly dressed in a well-cut suit and polished brown shoes. On his large square head he wore a little trilby hat, and a large cigar was balanced in the corner of his mouth. He puffed at it calmly, rarely taking it from his thick lips, even when he spoke.

Fred leaned on the greasy counter and yawned. 'Hello,' he said to the newcomer.

The other man grunted. 'Where are all those bleedin' kids?' he demanded.

Fred leaned down and from behind the counter produced Joe's brown leather briefcase. This he handed to the man while at the same time pointing towards the door where a terrified-looking Maisie stood next to her friend.

The beefy young man frowned and carefully opened the briefcase. Looking inside, he let out a loud roar like an angry bull. Swearing furiously, he tipped up the briefcase, scattering Joe's papers and exercise books all over the floor. 'What the hell has gone on? The job was called off because of the weather,' he yelled. 'Trust you stupid buggers to muck it up.' Red-faced, he turned to Maisie who was now cowering in the corner. Nosher backed away and moments later had roared off on his motorbike.

'I d . . . done it,' stuttered Maisie in terror. 'I fought he was the bloke, it was ever so foggy.'

'That's why the real geezer never came off the boat, you silly cow!' the man roared.

'Oh,' cried Maisie. 'Who was that bloke then?'

'Most likely to be a copper, you bloody fool. Where is he now?'

'Nosher's gone after him,' Maisie replied.

The man snorted. 'A lot of good he will be if the Old Bill are waiting down there. Now he's got the briefcase with all the money and we ain't got the dope. Come on, let's get him!'

The pathetic little blue exercise books of Joe's students lay face upwards on the dirty café floor as the burly man and Maisie ran like the devil was after them through the misty back alley-ways.

★   ★   ★

Joe trudged on. Ahead of him he could see traffic lights which indicated that he was approaching a main road. And now at last he could hear the distinct whine of traffic on the move. Too tired to think, he swung his briefcase as he walked. Thank God it was Friday. Tomorrow he could have a good long sleep and a lie-in. Perhaps he and Anne could go for a walk in the park . . .

But unfortunately for Joe, the night wasn't over yet. Suddenly he heard the roar of a motorbike travelling at high speed behind him. But before Joe had time to turn his head, a hand reached out and snatched the briefcase. The motorbike then roared off into the night.

Joe was astonished. He stood rooted to the spot, his mouth open but speechless. Moments later, he was attacked a second time. A burly man charged at him, knocking him off his feet and dragging him by the collar into a narrow opening between two high walls. Winded and shocked, Joe gradually realised that he was lying flat on the ground with something heavy pressed down on his chest. Looking up, he saw the burly man who was kneeling on him and holding a gun against his temple. Joe stared at the large head and mean eyes that glared at him.

'Cough up, copper,' a voice croaked. 'What's yer game?'

'Get off, if you want an answer,' Joe gasped.

The burly man got up, pulling Joe with him, and pushed him violently against the wall.

'I think Nosher got the briefcase.' Joe recognised the whining tones of Maisie.

'I'm not a policeman,' he said, his courage now returning.

'Well, what are you doing down here, then?' demanded the bully. He waved Joe's now empty briefcase in front of him.

'I got lost in the fog,' explained Joe. 'I'm a school teacher. Your little girlfriend picked me up and took me to the café.'

An image of the blue exercise books left back in the café flashed through the bully's mind. He looked worried. He was good with his muscles but in this sort of situation he was out of his depth. He turned to glare at Maisie. 'You picked up the wrong bloke,' he accused her. She was huddled against the wall, her blue eyes big with fright.

The bully suddenly lost all confidence. 'I don't know what to do,' he said, scratching his head under the small hat. 'You take care of him. I suppose I'd better run down to Queenie's and tell the Gaffer.'

'But what will I do with him?' demanded Maisie, pointing at Joe.

'Keep him until I come back,' the man growled at her.

'But he might punch me up,' whimpered Maisie.

The man sighed impatiently. 'Well, take the bleedin' gun, then, but be careful. Don't let it go off or you'll have all the Old Bill on the manor down here.' Dropping the briefcase, and handing his gun to the white-faced Maisie, the man slid off into the night.

Leaning against the wall, Joe was praying that this was not really happening. It all seemed like a corny movie. It had to be a nightmare. He rubbed his eyes with his hand and peered at Maisie.

A striking change had taken place in this woman. She no longer cringed and whimpered like a scared pup. Now she was all confidence. With one hand in her pocket and the other holding the gun, she placed a slim leg upon the low wall and said in a growl, 'Don't move, or I'll fill you full of lead.'

She sounded so absurd that Joe burst out laughing.

Maisie scowled. 'Shut up! What are yer cackling at?' she demanded.

'You, my dear,' replied Joe. 'Either that thing's not loaded or you've seen too many gangster films.'

Maisie smirked. 'Got a fag?' she asked. Joe handed her his cigarette case.

'Help yourself,' he said, 'then get my briefcase and allow me to go home.'

'Can't do that,' stated Maisie, lighting a cigarette and pocketing Joe's case. 'I got to keep you here till the Gaffer says what to do with you.'

'Now, Maisie, give me back my cigarette case,' said Joe, reaching out for it. 'It was a present.' He continued to hold out his hand but Maisie tossed her head defiantly and waved the gun under his nose as she moved a little closer. Joe could see right to the top of Maisie's black silk stockings. It was obvious that she was wearing nothing under the miniskirt.

'You ain't so bad looking for an old bloke,' she said, peering at him through narrowed eyes. 'Got any money?' she asked suggestively.

'Are you telling me that for a price you'll let me go?' Joe half smiled in a cold angry way. Inside he was hot with rage. It was ridiculous being held prisoner by this stupid chit of a girl.

'No,' replied Maisie, shaking her head slowly, 'I can't do that, the Gaffer would get me done over. As for you, he'd shoot your balls off!' She let out an unearthly cackle and poked the gun straight at Joe's groin.

This was the last straw for Joe. The rage boiled over. 'You bloody little whore!' Joe snarled. Feeling courage and strength surge up inside him, Joe let out a fist and punched her full in the face. Now Maisie went down like a sack of spuds. The gun went off with a loud bang and fell clattering to the ground.

Looking down at Maisie as she lay on the dirty

ground, her mouth open and eyes closed, Joe felt ashamed. She was a woman after all. He bent down and was about to pick her up when the sound of footsteps running in his direction alarmed him. This was too much. With a sudden panic, Joe bounded over the wall into someone's back garden. He then clambered over several more fences until he finally reached the main road. Ahead of him were those welcome traffic lights. At last his luck had returned. An empty taxi was waiting for the lights to change. Breathlessly, Joe threw himself into the cab. 'Baker Street,' he said, falling back into the seat with relief and exhaustion.

Chapter Two

British Justice

In the pinky-grey light of dawn, Joe paid off the taxi driver. He could barely keep his eyes open as he climbed the stone steps of his lodgings. He had become like a damned dormouse, he cursed himself. He used to be able to stay up studying all night without any trouble. That was age for you. And if he could have kept awake on the bus in the first place, he would never have become involved with those young gangsters.

An image of Maisie lying on the pavement flashed before him. Joe was worried. She had only been knocked out, he was sure of that, but what would happen when her bully-boy colleague found her?

Shivering with cold and fear, he put his latch key in the door, and crept up the carpeted stairs, anxious not to wake the rest of the boarding house.

But Anne heard him. She had been lying awake worried, for it was not like Joe to stay out all night. Now she stood framed by the lighted doorway of her room. She was dressed in a blue dressing gown, her long blonde hair hanging free. Joe was pleased to see her friendly face after his ordeal. He was extremely fond of Anne. They lived in separate rooms in the house but there was a strong bond of understanding between them and their feelings for each other were much more than just affection.

'Whatever's wrong, Joe?' Anne cried. 'You look as though you've seen a ghost.'

'Fog held me up,' muttered Joe dejectedly. 'I'm going to turn in. See you tomorrow.' Turning his own door handle, he went straight into his room.

Anne watched him disappear into his room with concern. Joe looked ghastly, she thought. He ought to take a holiday. Perhaps she would get away at the end of term, and then they could take a trip to Scotland. That would restore them both. She quietly made tea and settled down to write her weekly essay. There was no point in going back to bed now. In her spare time from her teaching job, Anne was studying for a sociology degree and worked hard at her studies.

A couple of hours later, the essay finished, Anne was sitting on her sofa reading a text book. Suddenly outside her door she could hear the tramp of heavy feet on the stairs. That was unusual, she thought. In fact, there seemed to be a lot of activity out there for a Saturday morning. Something was going on.

Getting up, she opened her door and peered out. Two men in raincoats were knocking loudly on Joe's door, but there seemed to be no response from inside. Joe was sleeping a deep sleep of exhaustion. Anne could see a couple of uniformed policemen standing by the stairs.

'Can I help you?' she asked tentatively.

The men stopped banging on the door and looked at her. 'We wish to contact Mr Joe Walowski. We are police officers,' one of them said.

'I'll go in and wake him,' Anne said, her hand on the door handle.

But the detective pushed her rather unceremoniously away. 'Sorry, madam, that's our job. Stand back, he may be dangerous.'

Anne momentarily looked amused. Dangerous? Her Joe? What were they talking about?

Now the men had opened the door and entered the room cautiously. Anne followed them.

Joe had woken up and was sitting on the edge of his bed in striped pyjamas. He was blinking furiously, his hair flopping over his eyes. 'What the devil's going on?' he yelled. But as he did so, the policemen pounced and yanked him to his feet.

'You are under arrest!' cried one. 'Come quietly.'

Anne ran to him. 'Joe, Joe, what's wrong? Whatever's happened, my love?'

Joe smiled at her calmly. 'It's all right, dear, I know what it's about,' he said. 'Pass me my trousers and my shoes, will you?'

The policemen stood waiting while Anne helped Joe dress. 'I'll get a solicitor for you, Joe,' she said. 'What's all this about?'

'I'm cautioning you,' declared the detective, 'that anything you say will be taken down and may be used against you in evidence.'

'I know,' muttered Joe. 'Don't make such a song and dance of it. Let's go.'

Anne was very upset. She was weeping as she ran after the police. 'Please, what is it? Tell me what you are charging him with.'

'Murder,' replied the policeman gruffly. Anne closed the front door and collapsed on the stairs as her knees went weak under her. By now the rest of the household was awake. The other tenants came from their rooms to offer solace to her.

'Don't panic,' said one, 'get legal aid. The police can make mistakes, you know.'

Amid the babble of voices, Anne tried to think clearly but all the time a voice shouted at her inside her head – not Joe, quiet studious Joe. He would not get mixed up in anything shady.

Joe sat in a cell in the police station. Outside the early edition of the evening paper screamed its excited headline:

BLONDE GIRL FOUND MURDERED IN EAST END ALLEY.

The police were busy filling out forms. Within an hour Joe would officially be charged with murder. It was an open and shut case as far as the police were concerned. Joe had not been difficult to find. His briefcase had been handed in to the police, having been discovered beside the dead woman's body. Also on the body, in the pocket of the woman's black leather jacket, was Joe's cigarette case.

'Is this your property, sir?' the sergeant had asked him earlier.

'Yes, that's mine, and I can explain,' Joe replied.

'So you want to make a statement?' asked the policeman.

Slowly and in a nervous halting manner, Joe told of his strange adventure in the fog that previous night. 'I know I struck her,' he said, after he had described what happened, 'but it was a straight left on the chin. She was only unconscious when I ran away.'

The detective rolled his eyes. 'Don't play silly boys with me, guv'nor,' he said wearily. 'It was more than a slug on the jaw that killed that poor silly kid.'

Joe stared at him incredulously. 'You mean she is dead?' He could not believe what he heard.

Someone brought in a photograph. 'Come here, mate, take a look at your handiwork.' The photographs were laid out on the table in front of him. Joe stared down with horror at what he saw. There was Maisie, only just recognisable because much of her face had been shot off.

Joe gave a gasp of horror and covered his face with his hands.

'Not a pretty sight, is it?' declared the detective as he gathered up the prints. 'Take him down to the cell,' he told the two constables.

As the uniformed men took Joe's arms, he suddenly lost all control. 'I never did it, I swear it,' he screamed.

The sergeant nodded. 'That's all right, mate, you'll get a chance to prove your innocence. Now, take him away!'

Joe was remanded in custody for twelve weeks while the police made further investigations. Then came the day of the trial, and in spite of Joe's defence, it was a waste of time. Everything was against him. Fred the café owner had seen the defendant with Maisie that evening. That Maisie was a bad character, there was no doubt. She often picked up men and her activities included prostitution. Her ponce was Nosher and more often than not they mugged the client. 'Down there,' Fred said, 'you was like the three wise monkeys, see all, know all, say nuffink.' This remark raised a laugh in the court room but poor Anne sitting quietly in the public gallery did not smile. She stared over at Joe's worn face and inwardly cried. How could he have been so foolish as to get mixed up with such people?

The newspapers were having a field day. The headlines became more and more sensational:

SCHOOL TEACHER ON MURDER CHARGE.
PROSTITUTE SLAIN IN ALLEY.

And up there on the bench was the dreaded woman judge. She was small, stout, middle-aged and very hard looking. Anne scrutinised the formal wig and the brown eyes behind the steel-framed spectacles but felt hopeless. In the past she had always admired this woman, thinking how hard she must have worked to become a judge. But now she hated her. She held the life of poor old Joe in her hands and showed very little emotion.

The prisoner admitted attacking the girl but as his lawyer pointed out, there had been no blood on his clothes and no weapon had ever been found. The police did manage to trace Nosher but to no avail. Nosher was found in a coma beside his motorbike in Epping Forest and never recovered consciousness.

The taxi driver was produced as a witness for the police. He remembered Joe, he said, because he had had a job to wake him. 'Fell into the cab, he did,' he said, 'like the devil was after him, he looked so scared.'

Towards the end of the week as the trial dragged on, Joe had become increasingly withdrawn. He sat with his hands over his eyes and his elbows resting on his knees. He did not look about or talk very much to his lawyers. He just seemed to shut out what was going on about him. He had given up.

Anne was afraid for him, terrified that the fine academic mind was breaking under the strain. From across the room, she watched his lips move and knew he was reciting poetry as he often did in moments of stress. The great works of Shelley and Shakespeare would console him in these times, she knew. Joe had memorised many, many lines by those writers. But Joe was beaten, Anne knew that, and her heart ached as she thought what prison would do to him.

The jury had reached a verdict: not guilty of murder – well, that was a relief – but guilty of manslaughter. The judge passed the sentence. 'I have no doubt that the victim was of doubtful character, but that does not excuse her terrible death. That you were suffering from some obvious mental strain is plain to see. You are an educated man with no previous convictions and I do not believe that you are a great danger to society. But you must be punished for what you did. I sentence you to six years in prison for manslaughter and recommend that you take psychiatric treatment.'

It was over. Joe was taken off to the cells and Anne remained sitting in the court room long after the judge and jury had left. A happy phase of her life was over: her time with Joe, her fellow lodger, with whom she shared so many interests. Never again would they meet up to drink cocoa together in her room and discuss poetry late into the night, leaving her alert and stimulated as if she had been injected with some drug to excite the senses as well as the intellect. Never again. And what made her saddest of all was that the key piece of evidence against Joe was the silver cigarette case which had been found on the dead girl's body. This, the prosecution argued, was clear proof of Joe's guilt. He had been involved with a prostitute, got into an argument about payment, and killed her.

Anne did not believe that Joe had killed the girl, but she was puzzled and hurt by the fact that the cigarette case was responsible for nailing him. For she had given it to Joe for his last birthday and it had been intended as a memento of a glorious night of love they had enjoyed together. Now she wondered if their feelings had been mutual, and was puzzled about why he would go with a prostitute. But she knew that whatever happened she would always have a place in her heart for Joe.

Chapter Three

Inside

Life in prison remained unreal for Joe for all the time that he was there. He barely noticed the coldness of the nights in the grey prison cell, the mixed-up days, the characterless baggy uniforms, the taunting of his fellow prisoners. Joe ignored them as he ignored their mocking laughter. He plodded wearily from recreation to solitary, where eyes viewed him through a small hole in the door. One day he was attacked in the washroom. A violent blow struck him behind the ear and then he was pulled down to the floor. Heavy boots lashed at him and a gruff voice croaked, 'Do the dirty bastard! Shot a young kid, he did, just a girl.'

Joe tried to get up and fight back but blood filled his eyes and a numbness had descended on his face. Joe lay weeping and wallowing in his own blood, very aware of the presence of the owner of that gruff cockney voice. His name was Buttons and he was a barrow boy, his voice hoarse from calling out his wares. He had a sadistic sense of humour and Joe would always remember him in years to come as his persecutor. He never forgot Buttons.

But there were other, happier, memories, too, which kept him going. Some were vivid and comforting: Anne, cool calm Anne assuring him that all would be all right; or the funny, enthusiastic students in his class. But there was one other which came to him over and over again, one that he had forgotten until his first night in prison. He remembered hearing a voice saying, 'You take care of him. I'd better run down to Queenie's and tell the Gaffer.'

Joe was puzzled by these strange words. Why had he not remembered them before? If he had told his lawyer he might have been cleared of this manslaughter charge. Now, night after night he lay on his bed and these words were a rhythm in his head. The Gaffer and Queenie! Queenie and the Gaffer! On God's earth, if they existed, who were they? That they had brought him to this place Joe had no doubt, but what or who were they?

As time went on, Joe became more and more fixated on the people responsible for his plight. He vowed that he would get his revenge. As the weeks and months went by, Joe began to mutter to himself. His lips would move and his eyes would roll angrily as he rocked backwards and forwards on his bed. The eyes peering through the hole in the door would take in what was going on and a report would record that old Dr Joe's condition was getting worse. None of the doctors could agree about the deterioration of Dr Joe's sanity and none had recommended moving him to Broadmoor. Instead, they waited and watched until his beaten-up body was found in the toilets and he was moved to hospital. There, with a badly damaged eye, cracked ribs and all his front teeth missing, Joe was left in peace to recuperate while the authorities tried to decided whether to send him to an asylum or another prison.

The three months in hospital brought Joe back to reality. He had begun to go back to his books and take more notice of the world around him. Even though his sight had been impaired, he was fitted up with a suitable pair of spectacles and given a nice set of dentures. And all that on the social welfare, Anne was jokingly told when she was allowed to visit him. Anne had smiled sweetly, her eyes filling with tears. 'That's more like my Joe,' she said to him that day, but she was sad because she had bad news for Joe. She told him that the tittle-tattle about her and Joe had forced her to leave her teaching job. She had got her sociology degree and was now off to a post in a town up North. 'I'm sorry, dear,' she told him. 'I would have got a job in London if I could but it was impossible.'

Joe seemed uninterested. 'Not to worry,' he said with a shrug. 'I've still got five years to do. You should just get on with your life and not bother about me.'

'But I will, Joe,' she protested, 'you know I will.'

But Joe shook his head. 'Goodbye,' he said with a philosophical grin. 'Who knows where I will go from here?'

Not long afterwards, Joe left the prison hospital on his way to another prison in Hampshire. He was looking relatively well and there was even a wry twinkle in his eyes as he said goodbye to the nurses. 'They tell me the new place will be like a holiday camp,' he said, 'that it will be very nice.'

It was now early spring. More than a year had elapsed since Joe had received his sentence and some built-in strength allowed him to face the future of five more years in confinement with a better spirit. In fact, he was, in a strange way, rather looking forward to it. It would provide good authentic material for the books he wanted to write and recording his thoughts would keep him busy during the time. Joe stared out of the dark, barred windows of the Black Maria in which he was being transported. The spring sales were on in London. Women were queuing outside the big

stores and in the bright sunshine the streets were
bustling with people. Watching them from behind
his new spectacles as he passed by, Joe's keen eyes
picked each person out and imprinted him or her
clearly in his mind. *I'll make good use of it*, he thought.
*I shall write and perhaps even paint – such opportunities
may never come again.*

In South London, the police van stopped to pick
up another passenger who now sat crouched in the
back corner, his eyes still red with weeping. He was
a young man on the threshold of life. In his early
twenties, slim and fair, his large bony shoulders were
hunched in grief.

Joe looked at the young man, his mild blue eyes
smiling with sympathy. The young man looked back
in gratitude with red-veined eyes.

The Black Maria took them through the green
English countryside and across on the ferry to that little mist-covered island that has housed so many of our
male citizens. At dusk, the cell door clanged behind
him and Joe stood looking around the small square
that was to be his home for the next few years.

So far this place was a vast improvement on the
London prison. It was cleaner and brighter and the
inmates seemed younger, most of them in their early
twenties. Joe was old enough to be their father. He
looked at them with compassion. It seemed like
such a waste of humanity to have those shuffling
youngsters just sweeping the paths with brooms,
or standing idle outside the long wooden army
huts which were all painted a dreary battleship
grey. But the air was fresh and crisp, and the
screws were more amicable than those in London.
Well, so far so good, Joe thought, now determined
to make the best of his long confinement. *And,
who knows?* he thought with a sudden flash of

optimism, *they might even find out who did do in Maisie* . . .

In this more relaxed frame of mind, Joe lay on his hard bed and began to make the acquaintance of his cellmate, who happened to be the young lad who had travelled down with him. His name was John, he said, and he lay with his long slim figure stretched out, his arms behind his head, staring mournfully up at the ceiling.

'This your first time, lad?' Joe asked.

John shook his head. 'No, I did six months in Borstal before I was eighteen. This time I got two years, but what chuffed me most, mate, was that I never did anything.' He continued to stare at the ceiling.

'You mean you have been wrongly convicted, too?' Joe stared at him in surprise. 'The English police seemed to be making a habit of this.'

Young John grinned. 'Yeah, mate, but I was set up. I just fell for it, that's all.'

Joe sat up and looked intently at John. 'What do you mean? I don't understand,' he said, puzzled.

John stared at him for a moment and then burst out laughing. It was a hearty infectious laugh which made Joe's sad face crinkle as he laughed with him. 'Well,' declared the younger man, 'I got a right one here.'

And so began a companionship that was more like that of father and son than friends. Joe told John what had happened to bring him to this place, and John recounted his tale in return.

'I wouldn't mind if I had actually done something,' he said. 'I've been going straight ever since I got married. I've got a lovely wife and a beautiful little son aged four. What bothers me most now is that I left her pregnant. I feel terrible. How will she cope? She's not an ordinary East End girl,' he explained. 'She comes from a good home and she's been brought up very soft. It just worries the life out of me.'

Joe listened sympathetically. 'Life provides, son,' he said philosophically. 'Your wife will get the courage to face her problems. It always comes from somewhere.'

During those cold spring nights when the island was shrouded in a white mist, the two men talked in low whispers, each one reliving the world he had left behind. They worked in the fields all day and at night were unable to sleep because of their aching backs. But as they talked, their sore blistered hands and feet were forgotten.

Joe was fascinated to hear about the East End world that John had been brought up in.

'There's me and me two bruvvers,' John explained. 'Always one of them was away. I never remember a Christmas that me old man or one of me bruvvers weren't in the nick. Me old lady must have spent a fortune going back and forth to visit them or fighting to keep them out – those bloody crooked lawyers must have rooked her for hundreds. And you know how she got that money? She used to do two jobs – office cleaning in the mornings and a shift in the jam factory at night.'

John was a resilient man with a sense of humour which delighted Joe. They both turned the most awkward situation into a joke. They became very close and the two men formed a bond. The long days and endless nights were shortened this way.

Very soon John's tall figure had filled out from the hard work that developed his muscles, and those broad shoulders were no longer bony. John was a protector. He was always there if there was any trouble brewing for Joe. 'Leave our Joe alone,' he would warn, waving a big threatening fist at anyone who dared to interfere with Dr Joe.

This was the nickname Joe soon earned himself at the camp. There were so many illiterate young men who wanted to write to their loved ones, and who received letters they were unable to read, that Joe soon came into his own. For these lads, for a small fee he wrote beautiful love letters, even long poems. And with the power of the pen, he helped to sort out their domestic tangles. He also settled arguments that arose between the prisoners themselves. This often happened, perhaps over a film or a television programme. Joe's clear memory and great knowledge of books stood him in good stead and gave him an unequalled popularity amongst the other prisoners; little gifts and comforts often found their way into the cell for favours given.

Neither John nor Joe received any visitors. John's young wife was unable to travel because of her pregnancy and Joe's Anne was miles away. But Anne did write regularly, telling him of her new job and how she was settling in up North.

So the summer months passed by and autumn tints washed the countryside as the prisoners rode in the lorry back and forth to the farmland. Then the cold winter descended on the island which soon lay in the grip of a white silvery frost. The land was frozen, there was no more work on it from now on. The men were confined to minor domestic duties inside, as kitchen orderlies, for example, or sick bay attendants. Time hung heavy but the resourceful Joe obtained some paints and canvas from the screws, and began to paint. At first it was a country scene, of trees, birds and the bright tints of autumn. Then he painted the white cliffs and the blue gull-decked sea. Then, just before Christmas, Joe began a portrait of Marie, John's young wife. He did this by copying from a photograph John kept on the wall by his bed.

The other inmates were very interested in this painting. John stood at Joe's side boasting of Marie's beauty, of her gold hair, her blue eyes, that cute little mole on her chin and the slim swan-like neck. Never was a work of art gloated over as much as Joe's portrait of Marie. Slowly it took shape, and the sensitive mouth and the large sad eyes of John's Marie became the talk of the camp.

A few days before Christmas, John received a telegram informing him that he was the father of a baby girl. With a loud joyous laugh, he waved the telegram for all to see. Even the stern face of the guv'nor relaxed to share his pride and happiness.

'Finish the painting, Joe,' John begged. 'Marie will be coming to see me now that the baby's been born. I'd like to give it to her.'

Looking at John's fresh complexion, the glow of health upon his face and the white gleam of his strong teeth as he talked and laughed, Joe felt saddened by the waste. *What an asset such an intelligent young man could be to a run-down society. Instead, this happy youth has been shut away for two years, deprived of the family that he loves so much.*

Joe hunched his shoulders as his thoughts drifted back across the Atlantic to the neat little house in Boston, and to Mary, his religious little wife whose Catholic heritage came from Irish grandparents. Few were more devout than Mary whose greatest ambition had been to have a brood of children for the Faith. She had married Joe and been disappointed. After eight years there had been no family and Mary had become very depressed. She lit candles every day in church and prayed to the Holy Virgin for a child. And Joe who had loved her deeply, finally lost patience with her and walked out. And then in spite of her piety, Mary took a lover and the same year she bore a child. So Joe decided to leave America. It was better to disappear, he thought, than drag Mary through a divorce court.

His thoughts roamed over the past, his head dropped and he looked quite dejected.

'Cheer up, Joe,' John called. 'Have a roll-up.' He threw over the old bent tobacco tin which they both shared.

Joe caught it deftly and proceeded to roll a cigarette. 'You know, you're a lucky boy, John,' he said. 'Look after your lovely family and go straight when you get out of here. You don't want to waste your life in a place like this.'

John laughed. 'Not on your nelly. I'll see they don't get me any more,' he said.

John's wife Marie was attracting many male glances as she made her way to the mainline station. Those men admired her slim figure, her corn-coloured hair twined about her cheeks and the little red miniskirt which stopped half-way up her thigh. With long strides she pushed the little blue pram before her, her left arm weighed down by a heavy basket of baby accessories. As she walked, Marie was oblivious to the attention she was getting, and she would not have cared if she knew about it. For her head was in an excited whirl as she thought anxiously, *Must get that train on time. I wonder if little John will settle down at the neighbour's? Baby looks comfortable, but I do hope I'm doing the right thing. Two weeks old is very young to make this long journey.*

This jumble of thoughts ran around her head like a buzz of angry gnats. With determination, she pushed the pram through the crowd, her breathing slightly heavy. She was still unfit from having given birth so recently.

She reached the platform barrier, handed over her ticket to be clipped, and boarded the train with a

grateful sigh. Willing hands helped her aboard, taking
the basket and pram. Marie sank into the corner of the
compartment as the train moved slowly out of the
station towards Portsmouth where it would meet the
ferry to complete that long run to the Isle of Wight.

Will John be pleased to see me? Marie wondered. *Please
God let it be the same between us! Don't let this parting
destroy our love.* With her face pale and her lips drawn
in a tight line, Marie sat praying for help and courage
to face the ordeal of visiting her young husband locked
up by the state.

The journey was long and tedious and Marie was
silent most of the time. There were several middle-
aged women in the compartment who wanted to chat
and admire the baby girl but Marie was nervous that
they might find out where she was going. She dreaded
their knowing the truth, so great was her shame.

She could almost see their nosey minds working
when one lady asked if she was taking the baby home
to the island. 'No,' replied Marie, 'I'm going on a day
trip to Newport.' An embarrassing silence descended.
The ladies knew, of course, Marie could tell that.

So for the rest of the journey Marie sat forlornly
engrossed in her thoughts until the train pulled into
the ferry boat harbour. How would John look after
eight months in prison? Would he look ill? Would
he have lost that cheery sense of humour that she
had always found attractive and which had pulled
her out of so many dull moods? She would not be
able to bear it if he had become bitter or if he still
bore her a grudge. How stupid and obstinate she
had been, insisting on giving evidence, unwittingly
turning the trial against him. He had been set up but
she had ruined his chance of getting off. She shuddered
at the memory. It seemed a long time ago, all that. She
had grown up considerably in the last eight months.

The ferry boat shuddered as they glided towards the

misty grey island. Marie put out her hand to steady the
pram and a cheery voice beside her said, 'I'll mind her
if you want to get a cup of tea.' Turning to look, she
saw a fat untidy girl in a very short dress with a wide
smile on her broad face. 'Go on, love,' the cockney
intonation was so familiar, just like John's. 'The baby
will be all right with me. And don't look so worried,
we are all in the same boat . . .' The woman laughed.
'In more ways than one,' she added with delight at
the pun.

Marie thanked her politely. 'I'd like to go to the
ladies, and the baby will be waking soon. I need to
find some hot water for her feed.'

'Up in the tea bar, love, they'll give you some,'
replied the girl. 'Hop off and make yourself comfortable.'

Twenty minutes later, Marie returned feeling more
refreshed and much less worried. She had got some
hot water and made up the baby's feed. The friendly
young girl sat with her fat legs crossed pushing the
pram back and forth. Underneath the jolly expression
there seemed to be a wistfulness to the uneven features
of her face. 'Going to visit your old man in the nick?'
she asked Marie bluntly. 'I'm Maudie, by the way.'

Marie held the baby on her lap as she sucked lustily
at her bottle. She winced at Maudie's question and her
blue eyes glazed over.

'Oh, don't let it bother you, duck,' chuckled
Maudie, 'we're all going over to the island to see
our old men. I've done several trips already this year.
See them over there?' She waved to a small crowd of
smartly dressed young women talking and laughing
together. 'They're all going up to Parkhurst,' she said,
'long termers, their old men are. They'll be old ladies
by the time their men get out.'

Marie stared horrified at her companion. 'How long
have they to go?' she asked, wide-eyed.

Maudie squinted over at them. 'That blonde one there, that's Tilly and the tall dark one's Theresa. Both their old men got thirty years. Ain't you heard about them? Been in all the papers, they have.' Maudie continued in her cheerful gossipy manner, while Marie trembled at the thought of a thirty-year sentence.

'That other one,' continued Maudie, indicating another woman in the group, 'the older one with the two kids, well, she's only got another eight years to go. Her old man got fourteen, like mine did.'

Marie held her baby against her shoulder to wind her. She gently rocked her back and forth, and two tears trickled down from her wonderful blue eyes. 'They took your husband away for fourteen years?' she murmured. 'It hardly seems possible.'

'It's true, mate,' replied Maudie, a trifle less cheerful. 'Five years I've been coming back and forth to this flamin' island. Still, the worst is over and he might get parole . . .' She sighed. 'But I'm twenty-five now, and I'll be turned thirty when he gets home. I don't suppose I'll ever have any teapot lids then, I'll be too bloody old.' She looked sad and held out her arms for the baby. 'Let me hold her, love,' she said. 'I'm mad about babies.'

Sympathy welled up in Marie's soft gentle heart as she passed her baby over for this stranger to cuddle. With the tiny bundle nestling in this untidy girl's arms, Marie began to tidy the pram. Tears trickled onto the frilly white pillow, the immaculate little sheet, and the dainty patterned cover. Maudie's lack of children reminded her that she had not at first wanted this little one. But once she was born, Marie had been smitten and now nothing was too good for her. She felt very sad, too, at the thought that this little one was seeing her father for the first time and that she would be a little girl playing in the garden before her dad returned home again.

The long journey had become interesting to Marie, now that she had a new friend. She left the ferry with Maudie who pushed the blue pram with such care. Marie walked alongside, feeling a little tense as they neared their destination.

'Where do we get the bus?' she asked Maudie.

'No bus,' declared Maudie, 'we do it in style. We get a taxi there and back.'

'Isn't that very expensive?' Marie asked with concern.

'No, love,' said Maudie, 'we all chip in and travel in the taxi together. Come on and meet the other girls.'

The small party of smartly dressed young women stood chatting with the two taxi drivers. There seemed to be a lot of debate amongst them and a lot of giggling. Soon Marie was sitting in the back of a cab with Maudie and three other women all jammed in tight. The pram had been dismantled so that the carrycot part could be placed inside on their laps. The women all chattered at once as they admired the new baby and counted her tiny fingers.

Then began the final phase of the journey through green leafy lanes to the dreaded prison gates. Marie looked about her shyly.

'She's new,' explained Maudie to the others. 'Her old man's in for two and it's the first time she's been on a visit.'

Sympathetic eyes fixed on her. 'Ah,' said one, 'then it's the first time her dad will see her.'

The speaker was a dark young woman called Kathy. She had long black straight hair, and lovely sensitive brown eyes. She was as smart and neat as they all were. Marie felt immediately at ease with Kathy, there was something very nice about her. 'My old

man's just finishing five,' she told Marie. 'He'll be
home in the new year. Time flies once the first year
is over, believe me, and they seldom do more than
three and a half.'

Marie was amazed at the casual attitude adopted by
all these women. This was their life and these resilient
people turned this monthly visit to the prison into a
kind of jolly outing for the girls. It was not possible
to feel sorry for them and none of them seemed sorry
for themselves, anyway. Self-pity was a luxury they
could not afford. But how free and easy they were,
even in front of the taxi driver! Why, everyone must
know where they went each month; it seemed that no
one dreamed of keeping it a secret. For Marie, this was
a revelation. She had spent so many anxious moments
worrying about whether her neighbours would find
out that John was in prison. It had made her feel quite
ill. But none of these wives seemed in the slightest bit
worried. They talked and gossiped and took it all in
their stride.

'Where's Pam?' asked Maudie.

'In the other cab,' the woman called Theresa
replied. 'We bunged her in with Mrs Green and
the kids. She's a bit of a dope, and she annoys me
with all that talk about other fellas.'

'Don't talk about dope,' declared the forthright
Kathy, 'she's full of pep pills and that ain't all, heard
she got a coloured man, now.'

'Cor blimey!' said Theresa. 'Her bloke will go up
the wall if he ever finds out.'

Marie sat and listened to this lively gossip and found
herself fascinated by them all. She wondered how they
all lived and how they conquered the lonely nights.
Only one woman remained silent and that was Tilly.
Throughout the taxi ride she sat staring out of the
window. Her make-up was thick enough to disguise
a hint of tears, and her blonde hair was perfectly

set into tiny little curls which rolled down onto her forehead, and a hair piece trailed in long sausage curls down her back. Marie admired her and the smart pink suit Tilly was wearing, but the cold sullenness of the well-reddened mouth worried Marie a little.

Catching Tilly's eye at one point, Marie smiled at her. But those red lips only twitched and the false eyelashes closed like a venetian blind over her sad eyes.

They were now travelling along a road where high red brick walls lined each side. Barbed wire and huge sirens decked the walls. Maudie's fat elbow nudged her. 'That's Parkhurst,' she said. Marie shivered as she looked up at the walls. Brave men's hearts were breaking behind those walls, she thought sadly, minds were becoming deranged. What a dreadful place it was!

A large black rook sat high up on one of the walls flapping his wings and croaking loudly, as though boasting of his freedom, his ability to fly away. Tears pricked Marie's eyes. 'Now don't get depressed,' Maudie was telling her. 'It won't do a bit of good,' she continued, 'they like to see you happy. We all cry when we leave but keep your pecker up till it's over, love.'

With this good advice ringing in her head, Marie climbed out of the taxi, re-assembled the pram, and went through the gates with the rest of the visitors.

Once the women were inside the gates and had had their credentials carefully examined, they split up. Theresa and Tilly went off in one direction while Maudie, Kathy and Marie went in another. From the other taxi emerged the tall, willowy, dreamy Pam, and Mrs Green, a faded little woman with two children aged about seven and five.

Pushing her little pram, Marie went towards the visitors' room, her heart pumping like mad. What would John say? It suddenly occurred to her that he might not want his kid to visit him in the nick. Would he be angry?

Soon the prisoners filed into the room where Marie and the others were waiting. The men all looked the same in washed-out grey-blue dungarees, but to Marie only her John was there. He looked very fit and was tall and tanned and he still sported that cheery grin. Thank goodness he had forgiven her, and prison had so far not defeated him. They sat facing each other, baby between them, enveloped in their own private little world that no one else could enter.

The visiting time passed too quickly but Marie was relieved and contented to know that her John was looking so fit and well and even more importantly, that he still loved her. Although they had both been very shy with each other and had little to say, she knew nothing had changed between them. The screw had relaxed and allowed John to hold his baby high in the air for all to see and admire, and Marie had felt very proud of both her husband and their little daughter.

An hour later, they had to part once more. Marie felt distraught as she waved goodbye to John and left. Then the heavy gates were shut behind her with a resounding bang. Outside the other girls waited for Marie. Now they had red-rimmed eyes and sad faces. It seemed that most of their bright sparkle had disappeared behind those high red walls.

They took the taxi back to the station in silence but on the train going home, they all began to cheer up. Make-up was repaired, sandwiches and cans of beer were bought from the buffet car and shared out freely. Everyone became jollier. Even the gloomy Tilly was more sociable as they told jokes and tales of their past and recounted what they did when their men were home.

'How was he, then?' asked Theresa. 'It's always been the same, in and out, all his life, my old man. First it was six months, then a year. And every time he went I was in the family way. It makes you a bit hard and bitter, it does, having to keep the home going, working evenings, the kids driving you mad all day. And all for what? He goes and gets thirty years, and he won't never come out no more. I feel sorry for the poor old sod, that's why I come every month. Mind you, I wouldn't have minded except I never got a light out of it, I didn't. He had a fancy woman when he did that big job. Proper mugs, we are, us wives.'

Having made such a long speech, Theresa lit a cigarette and blew the smoke out of her nostrils in a little gesture of disgust, then went back to her can of beer.

Tilly had put a gentle finger on the baby's tiny hand. 'You're lucky, Marie,' she said quietly. 'I lost my little girl, and I'll never have any more. Not with Bert, I won't.' Tears began to form in her eyes again and Marie felt quite embarrassed. The hurt was so raw and near the surface with the glamorous Tilly.

Luckily the gossipy Maudie saved the situation. 'My fella knows your John,' she said. 'He told me that your John was innocent; he just got rowed in by those brothers of his.'

Marie blushed. She hated any mention of John's twin brothers who were notorious rogues in the East End. But the rest of the women gazed at Marie with more respect. 'Is that your name, love?' asked Kathy, 'Crayton?'

Marie nodded dumbly and blushed more. How she hated being connected with that notorious family! How often had she begged John to stay away from them?

Now little Mrs Green spoke for the first time.

Until now she had been constantly busy chasing her kids around. Now, she had one on either side of her, forcibly holding them still so they could not move. Mrs Green looked over at Marie. 'Hope they look after you all right,' she said in a croaky voice. 'Worth a few bob, they are, with all them gambling clubs they've got.' She looked almost envious.

Marie's lips tightened into an obstinate line. 'I don't have anything to do with them and I don't want to,' she declared angrily. The other women all passed knowing looks to each other and then went on with their cheerful gossiping, leaving Marie to relapse into silence.

Marie's thoughts drifted back to the days before her wedding, and when her devoted mother had had a nervous breakdown, so worried was she that Marie, her only daughter, was about to marry a boy with a record.

'But I love John, Mother,' Marie had assured her. 'He will go straight for me, I'll make him.' She could hear herself repeating those words like a mantra, and the answer her mother gave. 'I know, Marie, but you can't change someone's blood.'

Sadly, her mother was not here now, having died of cancer when little John was only six months old. Now there was only Marie and her lovely babies and her fine strong virile John who was shut away for two years.

Heading back to the suburbs on the tube from Waterloo Station, Marie felt tired and depressed. She was also worried in case the baby woke up for her last feed before she reached home. Accompanying her was Maudie, headed for Mile End. Maudie was still very chatty and eager to inform Marie of the personal details of the other women. She told her that Kathy had three children and that Mrs Green was a right nit. 'Let's her old man run her life from inside, she does. Did you see the suit she was wearing? Too short, wasn't it? She sends up to a club for it on the book, and sends it back after the visit. Then she gets another one for the next time.'

'Whatever does she do that for?' asked Marie in amazement.

Maudie rolled her eyes. 'So as to look as smart as Theresa and Tilly,' she said. 'Her old man tells her off if she wears the same suit every time.'

A smile appeared on Marie's solemn face. This chatter really amused her. 'I can't think how on earth they manage it,' she said. 'I can't find money for any clothes. I had this suit before I got pregnant.'

'Tilly's got a bit tucked away,' explained Maudie, 'and Theresa works in a dress shop. Old Ma Green gets them on the weekly, and me, I borrow from me sisters.'

'Kathy looked nice,' said Marie, getting into the swing of it, 'how about her?'

'Makes her own,' replied Maudie. 'Ah, here's my stop. See you next month, Marie, ta ta.'

Back home at last, Marie collected little John from the neighbours and fed the children in her little kitchen. Once they were bathed and tucked up in bed, she sat down, picked up her knitting and went over the day's events in her head. She had been relieved to see John looking so well. He was the same man she loved, still making jokes and able to make friends easily. And he still loved her. Why, he had even had her picture painted by an artist he shared a cell with, he had told her. He would be sending it to her next week. She was so touched by this. So there was no need to worry over her John, nothing had changed.

The knitting needles clicked furiously. Marie sat building up her little love nest with straws of courage, confident that time would bring him home again soon. She would live for that wonderful day.

Back in the prison, John lay on his bed staring dreamily up at the ceiling. 'Did you see her, Joe?' he asked.

Joe had seen Marie as he was sweeping the path. He smiled at the thought of the lovely young woman in her red skirt and the tiny baby in the small pram. 'Yes, I saw her as she left,' he replied.

John beamed with pride. 'Smashing, ain't she? Did you see that beautiful baby?'

Joe smiled beneath his beard. Young John was in Heaven having seen his Marie. Joe found himself thinking of Anne, and silence descended as both men dreamed nostalgic memories.

Chapter Four

Queenie

The spring passed and a very hot summer began. The outdoor working parties left the camp each day and returned hot, thirsty and weary each evening. The cells were stifling and the long nights hot and uncomfortable.

Marie's portrait had been completed long ago and despatched to its subject. It now hung on the wall of Marie's sitting room in the suburbs. Marie had sent Joe a sweater and a parcel of books in return. Joe had had many requests to paint other portraits but recently he had become very lethargic and rather lost interest in his hobby.

One hot night in June, John returned from the working party. Joe was rather disgruntled about the fence building task he had been assigned to, and he missed the company of young John.

'Here, Joe,' said John, 'some bloke keeps asking about you.'

Joe raised his eyebrows. 'That's a surprise. What does he want?'

'Wants you to paint a picture of his bird,' replied John.

'His bird?' Joe looked blank.

'Well, you know, his girlfriend. She's called Queenie,'

explained John. 'He drives me and all the other fellas mad boasting about her.'

'Queenie . . .' repeated Joe. His intelligent protruding eyes behind the thick lenses showed interest. Queenie – that was the name in the back of his mind.

'It's that big-shot mate of me brothers',' said John. 'They got him for dishonestly handling. But believe me, Joe, there ain't no racket that the old Gaffer ain't involved in. He's got a finger in every pie.'

Joe's face paled. 'Did you say the Gaffer, John?'

'Yes, it means Guv'nor. He's a Geordie, and real right bastard he is,' said John.

'Queenie, the Gaffer,' Joe muttered to himself.

'What's up, Joe?' asked John, puzzled by the strange expression on his friend's face.

'How long has he been in here?' asked Joe.

'About two months,' said John. 'He got five years.'

'And this Queenie, where does she come from?'

John snorted. 'Everyone down the East End knows her. A proper bloody floosie, she is. Got a bar called Queenie's down in Stepney where I used to live.'

With a grim look Joe sat silent for a while as he took in this new information. Perhaps it was going to be possible to clear his name . . . First he would agree to paint Queenie's portrait. 'If you get Queenie's photograph from the Gaffer, John,' he said, 'I'll paint her portrait for him.'

The very next evening Joe started on his portrait of Queenie. He had studied the photograph very carefully, noting the mean narrow eyes which were wide-set and gave out a curiously provocative look. Appraising the small stocky body above long well-shaped legs, Joe was pretty sure Queenie had once been a stripper.

According to John, Queenie rose up from the ranks in the arms of a police superintendent who had frequented the backstreet clubs. Joe painted for hours and when he added the details of the hard little mouth and the high cheekbones, he felt an insane desire to slash the canvas with his paint knife. But he restrained himself and painted on.

After a few weeks, the painting was finished. Joe stepped back with narrowed eyes to survey it with a critical gaze. He then painted the background, a bar scene, with a line of neon lights and bottles. Then over the bar stool he painted a deep blue velvet cloak, and upon the blonde head, the royal crown. He then stepped back to view the portrait with a broad grin. The bar room Queenie had become the Queen of England. The small mean face stared out from its royal regalia. Joe felt very pleased with himself.

But John was horrified. 'Gawd,' he cried, 'what have you done, Joe? This is bloody treason! What's the Gaffer going to say?'

But Joe ignored him. He sat looking at the portrait with a wild look in his eyes. 'Makes a nice queen, doesn't she?' he remarked.

But John was worried. 'Christ!' he said. 'What if the Gaffer gets his boys to do me?'

With soul–destroying boredom, the weeks and months ticked by. Having been inspired by doing the portrait of Queenie, Joe now seemed to lose all his energy again. He stopped painting altogether and became bored and moody. He spent many hours just staring into space until John said, 'You are getting to be a gloomy bastard. What's up, Joe?'

Joe shook his head. 'Don't worry over me, kid, I've got things to work out. It needs a lot of concentration.'

'What things?' demanded John.

Joe smiled wryly. 'I have to think how I'm going to sort out my life when I get out of here.'

John sniffed. 'Well, that should be the last of your worries, mate,' he said, 'a clever bloke like you. Me, I've got nothing, only hard graft and a family to keep when I get out.'

'Sorry, mate,' Joe apologised. 'I'm a bit of a dead beat, I know. You can take Queenie's portrait over to the Gaffer any time you want now, John. I'm ready to let it go.'

'So you *have* finished that bleeding picture?' said John. 'About time, that's what I say. Every time I go over A Block the bloody old Gaffer sends for me and asks for it. To tell you the truth, I'm more than a bit scared of what he'll do when he sees how you decorated his bird.'

Joe nodded.

The next day, John came into the cell beaming. 'The Gaffer's gone into the top security nick,' he said. 'There's been a bit of trouble. I can't get the painting to him now, but his mate said I should take it to Queenie's myself if I get some parole. And with a bit of luck, I might. Marie's doing her best to get me a weekend. I should know by next month.'

Joe was interested. 'Where is this place?' he asked.

'Near Tower Bridge,' replied John. 'It's a big pub on a corner, you can't miss it. There are more bloody jobs pulled down in Queenie's than in the whole of the rest of London.'

Joe looked thoughtful. 'I wonder what role Queenie had in the crime I'm supposed to have done?' he said. 'You know, I sit here thinking about how to clear my name . . .'

John shook his head. 'Well, don't be such a fool,' he said. 'You've done more than half your porridge, now, so forget it. Everyone knows you was set up. Knuckles O'Leary was the bloke who carved up that kid.'

Joe stared at him in astonishment. 'Are you saying

that it's generally known that I was innocent of the crime?'

John looked embarrassed. 'You can't keep nothing from the grapevine, Joe, but it's better to let sleeping dogs lie. There's nothing you can do. And the Gaffer is still Jack the Lad, wherever he is. You can get your throat slit here as anywhere.'

The jubilant John got his weekend's parole. He left looking spruced up and tidy, and at the bottom of his suitcase was the portrait of Queenie and written permission from the prison authorities to take it to London. Joe spent the weekend feeling slightly uneasy about what Queenie's reaction would be when she saw the portrait. And he did not fancy crossing swords with the Gaffer whether inside prison or not.

But he need not have worried. On Sunday evening, John returned from the weekend with his family looking happier than he had ever been. He was full of plans for the future and love for his lovely wife and fine children. He told Joe that he had delivered the picture to Queenie with some trepidation, but she had loved it.

'She gushed over it, mate,' he told Joe. 'She said, "That's just like me old Gaffer. He always said he'd nick the crown jewels for me if he had to, that he'd put the crown of England on me head. And now he's done it." '

Joe stared incredulously at John as he recounted the conversation with Queenie. 'You mean she liked it?' he said.

John nodded. 'Wallowed in it,' he said. 'She's as vain and stupid as they come, and not going short of the other, I'll tell you that. She's got a guardsman sergeant kipping down in there.'

Joe smiled and looked thoughtful. 'Sounds interesting,' he said. 'I'll be visiting Queenie when I finally get back up to the big city again.'

Chapter Five

The Release

The festive season had started and the usual treats were put on for the prisoners – carol services and extra film shows. It was an especially good time for Joe, as his sentence had been cut short and he was being let out for good behaviour. It was the second Christmas at the camp for Joe and John. The spring would bring about their release. John became quite affected by the sentimentality of the occasion.

'Funny, ain't it, Joe,' he said on Christmas Eve. 'I'm laying here imagining myself dressed up as Father Christmas – red cloak, whiskers, the lot . . .' He began to sing a little tune under his breath – '*I saw Mummy kissing Santa Claus, underneath the mistletoe last night.*' Then suddenly his voice cracked. John turned towards the wall and covered his eyes. Joe knew that young John was weeping. He walked over and sat beside him, gently pulling the rough grey blanket around him.

'It's worse this year, Joe,' wept the lad. 'I keep thinking about the kids not having any toys.'

'Nonsense,' said Joe. 'Marie will look after them. She'll manage. And you must look on the bright side. Just think – this will be the last Christmas when you are separated from your family. Next year and the year after that and the year after that you'll all be together . . .'

Back home in London, Marie sat watching the telly. Both the children were upstairs and in the corner of the sitting room there was a small Christmas tree, with glass balls which twisted and turned in the firelight. Marie was feeling very sad and lonely. The Christmas programmes on the telly with their air of festivity made her feel more desolate. She would be so glad when Christmas was over. Last year it had not seemed so bad. She had had the baby and little John was at her mother's. This year they were an incomplete family unit, like a puzzle with a piece missing. At ten o'clock she was just thinking about going to bed when there was a knock at the front door. Marie jumped at the noise and nervously called out, 'Who's there?'

A merry voice replied, 'It's bloody Father Christmas, who do you think it is?'

Marie recognised the voice immediately. She laughed and opened the door. There on the step, heavily laden with bundles, was the fat untidy shape of Maudie.

'Merry Christmas, Marie!' she sang, exuberant and merry after her office party. She bustled into the house and started to unpack the bundles in her arms. 'You know,' she said, 'not another bloody Christmas Day will I spend in bed too sloshed to get up. And if I had some kids I'd give them a good time.'

'Oh, Maudie!' Marie's cornflower-blue eyes glowed with pleasure. 'I'm so glad to see you.'

Marie and Maudie had become close friends during their monthly trips to see their husbands. They chatted and giggled as they filled up the little pillow slips with toys and celebrated the evening with a bottle of cooking sherry.

Maudie stayed the night. The next day they all ate

Christmas dinner. It was only pieces of fried chicken
with baked spuds and tinned peas, followed by jelly,
custard and cakes, but it was delicious. It was a happy
day, Maudie was full of beans and great fun. She
played with little John, rocked the baby to sleep
and when the day was over and the children tucked
in bed upstairs, she and Marie settled down beside
the fire talking of their old schooldays and of their
husbands shut away by the state. The quiet, reserved
Marie and the rough and uncouth Maudie both found
something in each other. Their friendship was to be a
lasting one.

Spring arrived and with it came the day of their
release. Joe and John climbed off the train at Waterloo
Station looking somewhat confused and dazed. There
was nothing extraordinary in their appearance. An
observer might think them father and son, perhaps.
The older man was shabbier in an old-fashioned
tweed jacket and grey flannels which were baggy
at the knees. They both had the same lost expression
as though they could not believe that their release had
happened.

John spoke first. 'Let's go and have a beer, Joe,' he
said. 'I've forgotten the bloody taste of a Watneys,
I have.'

The two men went towards the buffet. Outside was
a telephone kiosk. 'You get the drinks, Joe,' said John.
'I'll phone Marie to meet me at the tube station.'

As John went off to make the call, Joe wandered up
to the bar in the refreshment buffet. The barmaid had
a sharp face and long nose. Her black hair was scraped
back into a ponytail. 'Yes, sir?'

'Two beers,' said Joe in a voice that seemed remark-
ably loud even to himself.

'Bottle or draught? Dark or light?' The barmaid
asked briskly as she wiped the top of the bar.

'Oh, a bottle, I suppose,' he said slowly.

The barmaid sighed and produced two bottles. She quickly took off the tops, poured out the light frothy beer and filled two glasses to the brim. Joe watched – entranced. The smell of the beer made him lick his lips. He had never fancied the drink so much before.

'Thirty pence,' barked the barmaid.

Joe fumbled in his pocket and from the few coins in there produced three shillings, which he placed on the counter.

The woman stared at them. 'Do you want one beer or two?' she asked sharply.

Joe suddenly began to feel very embarrassed. Something was wrong, he had made a mistake somehow. In confusion he stared miserably down at the beer and then down at the three shillings on the counter.

'I said thirty pence,' said the barmaid. 'That's only enough for one.' She seemed to sneer at the money in front of her.

Joe started to mutter apologetically when John's smiling face was suddenly beside him. John threw three more shillings onto the counter. 'Here you are, Old Mother Hubbard, don't do your nut.'

The barmaid snatched the coins with a sour expression on her face and went off mumbling.

John and Joe sat in a corner and drank their beer. It went down fine. 'Don't look so worried, Joe,' said John. 'It's not your fault that they changed the bleeding money system since we was inside.'

Joe suddenly understood. 'Good God, I forgot entirely about the decimal system,' he said.

'Then you'd better remember,' said John. 'You've got to pay double for everything. I just hope we're going to get double wages, too.' The good humour returned. 'Where are you going from here, Joe?' asked John. 'Why don't you come with me till you get settled?'

Joe shook his head. 'No thanks, John, I'll be all right. I might look around the town first.'

'Now watch it, mate,' warned John. 'Don't get into more trouble. You've done your porridge, now let sleeping dogs lie.' John's fresh face looked earnestly at Joe. 'Don't go getting mixed up with the Gaffer's lot, it ain't worth it, Joe.'

Joe grimaced. 'I can't promise you that, John, but I'll phone you in a few days.'

'As for me, I'm staying out of Stepney now,' said John, 'it only got me in trouble and I've promised Marie I'll go straight.'

'That's my boy!' Joe gave his young friend a warm handshake. 'Now, I'll be okay but just tell me what train I get for the East End.'

John sighed. 'All right, mate, it's your pigeon. Cheerio, look after yourself.'

With a last handshake they parted. John to his suburban home and family, and Joe back to that spot where it had all begun three years and four months ago. *Nick the crown jewels for you, I would, me love* . . . Joe smiled as he remembered the Gaffer's vow to Queenie, and he was more determined than ever to meet the Gaffer's famous woman.

Chapter Six

Down Fate's Highway

As Joe stood on the escalator going down to the platform in the tube station, he felt possessed by a sense of loneliness. From now on all decisions had to be made by himself – when to eat, when to drink, how to keep clean and warm. Everything had been provided for him while he was inside and he had become used to not having to think for himself. Now he was out, it was like being reborn.

This moving staircase could be transporting him straight down to hell. Who would know and who would care? The future looked bleak. Anne had not written to him for some time, and who could blame her? Teaching was finished. He would never get another job doing that. All the hard work to get those qualifications had been wasted. He'd probably end up in a city office licking stamps. All these gloomy thoughts raced around in his head. Oh well, he would let the hand of fate guide him. But first he would go back to the spot where it all began that foggy night.

With his parcel tucked firmly under his arm, he left the train at Aldgate and crossed the road, heading in the direction of the river. The road became very narrow and barely seemed wide enough to take the numerous heavy lorries which rumbled past. The houses around were mostly unoccupied, their doors and windows boarded up. And there was a curious absence of people in the street.

Unknown to Joe, this was the famous Ratcliffe Highway, the rendezvous of homecoming sailors, home of pimps, prostitutes and thieves. It was completely deserted in the day. Now down here was the café where Joe had met Maisie. Two white-turbaned Indians passed him, lost in their dreams of the East. Joe walked on and then suddenly like an oasis in a desert, Tower Hill appeared before him. The Tower glinted in the sunlight, and beyond it was the magnificent structure of Tower Bridge spanning the great river. Cars swirled noisily around a traffic island. Joe smiled. The drastic change of scenery momentarily delighted him.

He strolled onto the bridge and leaned on the parapet to look down at the deep dark river flowing swiftly beneath him. The traffic rumbled heavily across the bridge and little waves of the Thames dashed against the muddy foreshore as the tidal river rushed down to the sea. Despondency had left him. Joe was suddenly filled with a great desire to paint the ivy-mantled towers and the cool grey sweep of the river as it wound its way eastwards. He felt strong and clear-headed. No, he would never give in. Somewhere in that little maze of back streets was the secret of his downfall. Whatever lay ahead, triumph or disaster, he would treat these two imposters just the same and press on with his mission. He had to find the bar that Queenie owned, but that would not be difficult if he followed young John's directions.

He walked past a long line of wharves and came to a street with terraces of working-class houses. And there, standing prominently on the corner, was a large Victorian tavern. It was tall and gloomy, with high brick chimney stacks and beams of dark wood.

Walking towards it he could see the stark black letters over the glass door – Queenie's Bar.

Joe's heart was racing as he came closer. After a moment's hesitation, he pushed open the door and went inside.

In contrast to the gloomy outside, the inside of the pub was luxurious. Joe was struck by the brass-topped tables, the red pile carpets and purple velvet drapes. Little red-shaded lamps around the room created a warm, rather mysterious atmosphere.

On the customer's side of the bar counter sat a pretty little blonde woman perched high on a stool. This had to be the famous Queenie. After painting her portrait, Joe would have recognised her anywhere. She was wearing a very short black dress which showed off her long legs clad in flash nylon tights. She had full red lips and a pert nose. Queenie was sitting cross-legged with her elbows on the bar. Through a veil of long false lashes, her eyes surveyed everybody and everything, missing nothing.

Joe suddenly felt very strange and unguarded. Having reached his destination, a kind of weariness came over him. Slowly he walked towards the polished bar, put down his brown paper parcel and fumbled in his pocket for money to buy a beer. A pleasant young barmaid served him. Queenie did not move from her spot. She sat on her high stool, chin in hand. Joe could almost feel those eyes fixed on him, watching his every movement, never missing a thing.

He turned and smiled at her. Queenie did not respond but her beady eyes transferred their gaze to the brown paper parcel under his arm. 'Just get out?' she asked. Only her lips moved. Her voice was soft, charming and pleasant.

Joe was quite taken aback by the question. He

was too shocked to deny it. 'Only this morning,'
he answered.

'Scrubs?' she asked. It was more of a statement than
a question.

'No,' replied Joe, 'The Island.'

There was still no change of expression on her face
but she looked at an expensive diamond watch on her
wrist. 'It's nearly time,' she said. 'Wait till I close the
bar and I'll give you some lunch.'

The offer was made in a generous manner but she
did sound as though she did not expect to be refused.
She slid down from the high stool and rubbed her
elbow as though it was cramped. She was not very
tall but her figure was neat and her walk slinky and
very sexy.

'Sit down,' she commanded, directing him to a
small room at the back of the bar that had several
tables covered with checked cloths and tastefully
arranged vases of spring flowers. 'I'll get you some
lunch and then I'll come and have a chat with you
when I've checked the till.' She spoke in the same
warm responsive manner but it was very authorita-
tive. It was as if her word was her command.

Joe was rather astounded by the charm of this
Queen of Stepney. She was so different to anything
he had imagined.

For lunch Joe was served with roast beef and veg-
etables, jam pudding and custard. His beer glass was
refilled whenever it was empty. It was a very filling
and tasty meal. Queenie joined him with the coffee.
She sat down and offered him a cigarette. She lit one
for herself and settled down for a little chat. Joe could
not believe that his luck had held out for so long.

'I expect you were hungry. Feel better now?'
she asked.

Joe's mild blue eyes looked through his thick spectacles straight into those hard little bright button eyes

of Queenie's. A curious shiver went through him and he realised that he was attracted to her. She certainly excited him. He noticed the heavy gold chain she wore about her neck, took in the soft white skin, the slim-fitting black skirt. He observed the heavy charm bracelet that dangled from her arm as she moved, the various rings on the white hand. She was certainly smart and very expensive. And she was as alert and shrewd as a wild thing. A real vixen was the Queen of Stepney.

'How did you know I was an ex-con?' Joe asked politely.

Queenie smiled scornfully and looked down at his brown paper parcel which rested on the floor. 'Seen too many of those in my time. Most of the ex-cons begin and end down here.' As she spoke, she looked at Joe very carefully. 'And did the Gaffer give you a message to bring?'

Joe looked back at her with caution in his glance.

'It's all right,' she said reassuringly. 'You must be the old guy who painted the picture.'

Joe was quite offended by this. Old guy? What a cheek! And she was no spring chicken herself!

Amused by his indignant expression, for the first time Queenie laughed, letting out a kind of warm, throaty giggle which was rather attractive. 'Don't get shirty,' she said. 'I didn't mean old in that respect. And the portrait was lovely. But when they told me old Dr Joe had painted it, I thought you must be about eighty. Actually you're not so bad.'

As she leaned forward, the smell of violets wafted across the air. Joe realised that the sexual urge, which had not bothered him for a long time, had become very urgent indeed. And Queenie knew.

A mischievous glimmer came into those beady eyes. She got to her feet and stretched slowly. 'I suppose I'd better get to bed. I always have an afternoon rest. I need to since I don't get to bed until the early hours in this business.'

Joe hesitated. Was this an invitation? He dared not believe it. He picked up the tell-tale parcel and rose to his feet. 'Well, I'd better be going. Thank you for the lunch.'

'Okay,' she replied nonchalantly. 'Pop in again sometime.' Then with a quick movement, she was standing very close to him and looking up with her dark eyes. 'Don't be such a chump,' she whispered. 'You need it as bad as I do.'

Two arms encircled his neck and her soft body pressed close to him. Joe was lost. Never before had he experienced such excitement. His body positively trembled as she touched him with her hands and their lips pressed together, tongues darting. The need was so great that neither of them could wait. They moved towards the small settee in the dining room. Queenie quickly slipped off her dress to reveal a compact white body now clad only in a brief bra and a G-string around her crotch.

'Come on, Joe,' she whispered, 'let's go up to bed and make love in comfort.'

And so in the frilly perfumed bedroom upstairs they made love fast and furiously. Then almost immediately, Queenie forced Joe to perform again. Afterwards she lay beside him silent and perfectly naked and looking satisfied as if she had just had an excellent meal.

Joe was very confused. Now sated, he pressed his face into the pillow. He felt almost ashamed, like a teenage boy who has just been seduced. He was usually quite romantic in bed. But this had been so casual. Queenie seemed to have no soul.

'Have a kip, now,' she said as she got up to go to the bathroom. 'I'll introduce you to the boys tonight.'

But Joe was already sleeping a sleep of exhaustion.

★　　★　　★

Joe was aroused later by a peculiar sound. It was a kind of high-pitched whine which stopped and started, stopped and started. Sitting up, he realised that it was a vacuum cleaner outside in the passageway. Through the doorway he saw a very fat lady manipulating the machine, pushing it along almost angrily. When she saw Joe, she turned it off. Red-faced and belligerent, she stared at him. 'Better get out of that bed,' she said. 'I've got to clean the room. Besides, the missus will need you downstairs. It's past six and time for the bar to open.'

Having delivered her ultimatum, the fat lady cast him another menacing look and slammed the door.

Joe did not think it was wise to stay in bed for much longer. He got out of bed and went to the bathroom. It was as luxurious as the bedroom, and full of sweet-smelling soaps and oils. Joe took a hot shower, dressed and then crept shyly downstairs to the bar.

Queenie was perched on the same stool in exactly the same position as she had been in when he first saw her. It was almost as though that afternoon had never happened. Perhaps it was indeed all just a bad dream . . .

She had, it seemed, changed her dress. It was another black one but this was velvet and full-length, and it had shiny beads on it. In her perfectly set hair she wore a jewelled clip. A queen indeed, she looked, but she was treacherous.

Joe walked towards her warily, unsure of the sort of reception he was going to get.

Queenie glanced at him. 'There's coffee in the kitchen,' she said coolly. 'Then if you don't mind, could you give the girls a help in the bar?'

Joe was bemused. Well it was not exactly a lover's welcome. He wondered where his parcel was – he thought that once he'd found it he'd leave. But in the meantime he would hang about here and see if he could learn anything in this place which was obviously very shady indeed.

Chapter Seven

Queenie's Court

Joe was still drinking his coffee in the kitchen when a coarse voice bellowed at him. 'The missus wants yer, mate. Yer got to help the girls behind the bar.'

Joe did not know who it was but he obeyed anyway, returning to the now very crowded and smoky bar. With a grim expression on his thin face, he began to collect the empty glasses and put them into a special machine that washed them. In no time he was expert at placing them into the small glass fountain, taking them out, polishing them and putting them back on the shelf.

At one point, as he held a tumbler up to the light, he beheld the incredible Queenie still sitting in the same position, with her face slightly flushed and her courtiers surrounding her. When she moved she was like a puppet on a string, with stiff movements. Occasionally, one white hand, with its diamonds sparkling, would slowly pour the tonic into the gin. She was looking at a large man who was engaging her in what first seemed to Joe to be a heated argument, so loud was the man's voice, so erratic his movements. But drawing nearer to get a closer listen, he realised that it was only a friendly discussion.

On the other side of the bar, the customers were a mixed group. There were young girls with long flowing hair and very short skirts, and strong young men with hair as long as their girlfriends'. Joe thought that it was not easy to distinguish between the two sexes. He industriously polished the glassware as he watched the floor show which had just begun. A robust and very immodest young woman stripped with a series of erotic wiggles to the strains of a popular song. The men all around leered at her and reached out to touch her until, finally, at the end of her act, clad in only two silver stars and a G-string, she fled to avoid the clamouring hands.

Joe viewed the scene with enjoyment. London had certainly taken on a new lease of life. No wonder they called it the swinging city now. Why, it was more like Paris or New York than that staid, respectable old lady he remembered.

Eventually Queenie reached out her arm and rather daintily pulled a brass ship's bell which hung over the bar. It was time. The customers began to leave.

It was then that the Queen finally left her throne to pull the velvet drapes over the windows to keep out inquisitive eyes. There were about twenty people left in the bar. Trays of food were brought in, drinks were passed around and the Friday night party had begun. Some young couples still danced very close together, but most people were sitting about talking and drinking.

Queenie turned towards Joe and for the first time that evening acknowledged him, fixing him with her bright beady eyes. 'Come on, Joe,' she called in a pleasant manner. 'You can relax now, we're having a party. Come and meet the boys.'

Joe wiped his hands on the towel and, still looking very subdued, joined the other guests.

Queenie was waving an imperious hand at three men who sat near. 'Meet Spinx, Doug and Spud,' she said.

Joe suppressed a smile. They sounded like a musical comedy team.

The three men looked up at him and nodded. 'Hello, mate,' they all said in unison. One handed him a drink, another a plate of sandwiches. Joe sat down and joined them all at the small brass-topped table and listened in amazement to their conversation. They talked fast and noisily, punctuating every sentence with four-letter words. It was rough, tough talk but had an attractive casualness to it, too.

'Cheer up, Joe,' roared the hefty red-faced man, giving Joe a violent thump on the back. He was Spinx, and the one they seemed to regard as the boss. 'We won't bite yer!' He had a mottled, weather-beaten look about him and rugged features which looked as though they were made out of granite. Watching him, Joe thought that the name Spinx seemed to suit him very well. Spinx had steely-blue eyes which shone like gimlets and seemed to bore through him. They did not smile but Spinx's wide mouth with its magnificent white teeth often broke into a jolly grin. 'I'm the big boss around here, while the Gaffer's inside,' he explained to Joe.

This was the first mention here he'd heard of their boss, the Gaffer. He pricked up his ears and listened all the more carefully. 'I only got out today,' he explained. 'It takes a bit of getting used to.'

'Yeah, it takes a bit of time, lad,' Spinx said reassuringly. 'I did a five-year stretch, meself.' He filled Joe's glass up to the brim. 'Get that down you, lad, it will buck you up no end,' he chuckled.

Joe gulped down his drink and there was a lull in the conversation until Spinx looked up over the bar and said, 'You old Dr Joe who painted that portrait of the Queen?'

Joe looked in the direction of Spinx's gaze and for the first time he noticed the portrait he had

painted of the Gaffer's Queen while he had been in
the nick.

Spinx was chuckling still. 'Don't arf fancy herself,
our Queenie,' he said with a hoarse laugh. 'But listen,
lad, if you can paint, you can also draw, so I might
have an interesting proposition for you.' He reached
for the whisky bottle and refilled the glasses as he
fixed his inscrutable eyes on Joe. 'I might have to
consult the rest of the boys but I think you could
be very handy.'

Joe was beginning to feel the effect of the alcohol.
His head spun a little as he drank his whisky.
Watching Queenie as she danced closely with a
long-haired boy, he realised that his hazy mind was
telling him to be wary. It seemed too extraordinary
that he should have fallen so easily into the arms of
the notorious Queen.

Thinking about Spinx's remark, Joe began to
wonder what they were cooking up for him. He
glanced back in the direction of the Queen of the
hive of crime. Her slim body swayed sexily from
side to side as she danced with the teenage boy. A
blonde curl had wandered from its clip and fallen to
lie on her bare shoulder. That she was an unscrupulous
bitch Joe was sure, but, God, what an effect she had
on him!

Spinx's voice became low and confiding in his
ear as he followed Joe's contemplative appraisal of
their Queen. 'Don't let her bother you, mate,' he
whispered. 'It's the cock she's after, not the poor sod
at the other end of it.'

From behind his thick spectacles, Joe's eyes assumed
a merry twinkle as he suddenly started to laugh
out aloud.

'That's it, mate,' said Spinx, refilling Joe's glass
once more. 'Enjoy yourself. All women are a bleeding
nuisance one way or another. I'm glad to have you

on the firm. We could do with some brains in this outfit.'

The whisky had taken effect completely. Joe felt very relaxed as he got drunk with Spinx and together they chattered about America. It turned out that Spinx had visited America while in the wartime Navy. They also talked about the Scrubs, the Island and various other prisons Spinx had resided in.

Spinx was surprisingly open about himself. He said he was a Londoner, born and raised a cockney (and proud of it) but now he lived in Essex and only came to town on business.

One of the other men, Doug, was a large, flat-nosed fellow with two cauliflower ears and speech that was decidedly slurred. He told tales of glory in the boxing ring and made many dirty jokes.

Joe listened to the man's patter but he could not concentrate on what was being said. He felt as though he were floating far away. Someone banged him on the back and shouted in his ear but Joe did not care. By now he had that pleasant swaying sensation of intoxication so he just closed his eyes and within moments had gone off into oblivion. He did not regain consciousness until the cold light of morning hit his face.

He had a strange heavy feeling in his arms and legs which made him wonder if he could lift them up. Opening his eyes he found that he was still in the lounge bar of Queenie's and he was lying stretched out on the red leather seat. Looking around, he saw other bodies there, lying on the floor. One he recognised from the night before, a young man in a dirty white roll-necked jumper. He was called Hustler. On the seat opposite lay his pal, Snatcher, whose mouth was wide open, his long hair flopping over his eyes. Under his long thin form stirred a dishevelled-looking blonde woman who was just disentangling her bare legs which had been in an obscene position under him.

Rather embarrassed, Joe staggered to his feet and went into the back room. Under the table he found the battered-looking form of Doug.

'Make some bloody tea, Joe,' the boxer muttered.

Feeling like a servant, Joe made a huge pot of coffee and handed out cup after cup. Half-way through his task, he discovered another blonde girl in an alcove in the kitchen. She wept when she discovered it was already morning.

'Ow,' she wailed, 'what's me muvver going to say?' But she found no sympathy with her friends.

'Shut yer bleeding mouth,' one of them shouted at her and the other seemed to agree.

Joe called a cab and loaded the overnight visitors into it. He was alone once more, now amid the debris of last night's party. Staring around at the shambles, he wondered vaguely what he had done with his brown paper parcel. He began to search for it, keen to retrieve it and get on his way. For the time being, he had seen and heard all that he needed to at Queenie's Bar.

His search was interrupted by the arrival of smiling little Nelly the barmaid. She looked fresh, sweet, and clean, with a little blue scarf tied around her mousey hair. 'Morning, Joe,' she said cheerily. Then looking around the room she exclaimed, 'Gawd what a bloody mess! Come on, love,' she said, 'let's get it sorted out before the missus gets up.'

Resistance was conquered. Joe was just putty in the hands of sweet Nelly and in no time he was back at work collecting and washing glasses and picking up chairs and broken bottles.

Nelly hummed a little tune as she wiped the tables.

'You look rough, Joe,' she commented cheerily. 'Don't suppose you got much sleep last night.'

The next arrival at the bar was someone called Beery Bill, and also the fat woman who had manoeuvred the vacuum cleaner so menacingly the day before. Swiftly and silently the team worked. Joe marvelled at their cheerful efficiency. They seemed like little cogs in a big wheel, their contribution vital yet their reward probably only a few pounds a week as they worked hard for their common interest – the missus and Queenie's Bar.

Not long after, a half-dazed youth staggered down the stairs, fumbling his way to the front door. Not a word was spoken but Joe noticed meaningful glances passing between Nelly and the fat woman, who proceeded immediately to lay a tray with a cup and saucer and a small pot of tea.

'Take the missus her tea up now,' Nelly growled.

Joe was still hard at work polishing the counter and then loading up empty bottles for Beery Bill to cart away. At one point Joe was horrified to watch Beery Bill pour several half-empty bottles of beer into one big pint glass and proceed to guzzle it down, wiping his thick whiskers with the back of his hand.

'The hair of the dog what's bit yer, the best drink of the day,' Beery Bill said with a satisfied burp.

Suddenly Joe wanted to heave. His stomach contracted and he felt the gorge in his throat. The smell of stale alcohol and all the rich food and whisky he had consumed the night before were all too much after the strict prison diet. His body rebelled. He dashed out of the door into the backyard toilet. There he retched for two minutes. Coming out, he felt much better but exhausted and subdued. In the yard, he was surprised suddenly to feel the rush of clean fresh air blowing past him and he realised that he was looking out at

Queenie's Castle

the river. Old Father Thames flowed directly past Queenie's back door.

Walking to the low wall, he leaned over to look at the misty morning river scene, taking in the shadowy spires and the tower on the other bank. His gaze followed the grey sweep of the river to where the thin shape of Tower Bridge crossed the water. There was no sun at all, just a flat grey sky. Storm clouds hung black and heavy on the skyline. They looked ominous but Joe beheld a sombre beauty in them, a still, brooding silence that seemed to make even that faint rumbling of the traffic momentarily still. After all the excitement inside the bar, this peaceful scene rejuvenated him wonderfully. He breathed deep, in and out, and his artistic soul soured as high as the heavens. He felt at peace.

Joe rested his arm on the wall and settled down to watch that ever-changing scene. A coal barge drifted slowly past, towing another. A man went by dreamily steering a small motor tug. Then a police launch appeared and disappeared, the mist began to clear and the funnels of the ships in the dock could soon be be depicted displaying little flags flying in the breeze. A large cargo vessel approached and Tower Bridge began to open to allow it to pass through.

Joe was fascinated by this morning river scene. He watched intently as the outgoing tide carried a large patch of black oil past him. Sweeping to the shallows, the oil collected the debris. Plastic bottles whirled round and round, an oil drum bounced on the water and slimy pieces of wood were caught up by the tide. There was a lot of rubbish, too – cigarette packets, newspapers and plastic cups, hustled and bustled down the tide, all held together by the patch of slimy oil. It was the filth and pollution of a city floating out to sea.

Watching it all go by, Joe suddenly felt like one of

those plastic bottles drifting on the tide. He did not know where he was going, he had to go with the flow, unable to resist. He had no idea where he was headed or in what situation he would find himself. *Go on, Joe*, a voice whispered in his ear. *Get out of here or you'll be in trouble . . .*

Joe momentarily looked about him, but he knew that the voice came from inside him.

His reverie was interrupted by the loud voice of Beery Bill who had come into the yard wheezing horribly. 'Give us a hand down the cellar, Joe,' he called. So Joe, with a nod of assent, followed the man down the rickety wooden stairs to move the heavy jars and barrels. Queenie's kingdom must continue to function.

Chapter Eight

The Office

A few days later, the thoughts in Joe's head were still very confused. Why could he not make up his mind about what to do? Why was he feeling utterly stymied? Why had he really come here in the first place? Was it to prove his innocence? Was it really, when he doubted if he had a hope in hell of doing that? Young John had probably been right when he had said that it was better to let sleeping dogs lie. Having spent what seemed a lifetime at Queenie's Bar, even though it was a mere four days, he had the strong conviction that everyone there was fully aware of his being set up in the first place.

So far he had been treated very well, as though he were truly part of their close community. He had been well fed and well bedded, just like a stray donkey, stabled and fed. In a way the place reminded him of prison, what with the regularity of the opening and closing hours, the number of chores to be done, the precise times for eating and sleeping. It was indeed like prison but obviously a lot more comfortable. And he did know why he was still there. He had hung around because he thought that someone would show his or her hand at some point and lead him to the person who *did* murder Maisie.

While turning over these thoughts in his mind, Joe

was eating an excellent lunch cooked by Nelly Green. Nelly's face was red and hot with perspiration from the heat of the oven. Her small hands were rough and chapped from the harsh effects of detergents and hot washing-up water.

Nelly did not eat. She sat opposite Joe and drank a cup of strong tea. 'Don't feel like a lot to eat after you've cooked and served it all,' she commented, as she did every day.

Joe looked directly into her brown eyes that seemed to twinkle all the time. The deep lines around her eyes and silver streaks in her light brown hair bothered him. 'You work much too hard, Nelly,' he said.

'Got to, ain't I?' returned Nelly in a matter-of-fact tone. 'Welfare money won't keep us. I've got three kids, you know, Joe.'

'You look too young to have so many kids,' he said respectfully, causing Nelly to giggle like a young girl.

'Get away!' she said, pulling at the sleeves of her faded cardigan as though to hide the red roughness of her arms.

Joe smiled at her. He liked her a lot and admired her toughness. She was as cheery as the proverbial cockney sparrow, whatever her dire circumstances. 'Are you a widow, Nelly?' he asked.

'No, of course I ain't!' She gave another little titter. 'Me old man's inside. Done four, got two more to do.'

Joe looked sympathetically at her, but he knew that Nelly did not need sympathy when she began to give him a long, detailed account of having been on a visit to the prison, of how smart she and the children had looked.

'Get it all on the weekly,' she announced triumphantly. 'My Bill likes me to look nice, and while I've got a pair of hands to work my kids don't want for nothing.' A charming smile lit up her faded features, revealing a hidden beauty.

Joe admired her confidence in her own ability to cope with her hard life. He put out his hand and squeezed her rough red hand with its broken fingernails.

Nelly pulled away. 'Now stop it, Joe,' she warned. But Joe knew that a bond had formed between them – one that might prove very useful to him in the future.

It was not long before Joe discovered that Beery Bill also had a prison record. He told Joe that he had done more time for petty larceny and for being drunk and disorderly than he could remember. He had been in and out of prison all of his life, until recently when he had finally decided to go straight and keep out of trouble. 'Don't want to die in the bleeding nick,' he informed Joe. His bleary eyes looked out forlornly from an age-lined face and his grey moustache was tinged with permanent brown beer stains.

Another member of Queenie's staff was Fat Lot, the large woman who growled occasionally but otherwise had little to say. She swept, cleaned and vacuumed most of the day with extraordinary vigour. She had been christened with the lovely name of Charlotte but was known to all and sundry as Fat Lot. Joe soon learned that the last of her large brood of sons was doing his initial training at Borstal and her husband had lost his life at sea.

So it was among members of this fraternity that Joe found a home. Gradually he came to believe that all his sober, serious acquaintances of the past had none of the warmth and humour for him that these East-Enders offered him. They made him laugh and the melancholy that had always possessed him seemed to disappear. These people had frankness and honesty about them that was very refreshing. He felt quite different when he was with them. He remembered how ill at ease he had been with the rest of the teaching staff at the college where he taught, and he decided that, apart from Anne, he thoroughly disliked most of the English with their snooty ways and smug respectable conversation. But these East-End characters were different. They laughed, drank and worked, swore and fornicated all in the same easy-going manner. Joe Walowski liked them very much indeed, even though it was their type that had landed him in trouble in the first place.

It was striking to him that no one ever asked him any questions. It was almost as if they all knew his fate, as though they were just watching a man about to be hanged. And Queenie too was a mystery to him. Every now and again Joe caught her small bright eyes surveying him in a thoughtful manner but since that afternoon session, nothing had happened. It was extremely puzzling. But he did not try to make contact with her. Instead he went about his work, methodically polishing glasses and stacking bottles, waiting and waiting for something to happen, as surely it would.

One evening Spinx's hefty shape appeared at the bar. He was well dressed in a light suit and fawn cap on his large head. 'I'm going up to the office,' he muttered to Queenie. 'Send up old Dr Joe, will you?'

Queenie shifted on her stool. 'It will be handy having a doctor on the firm,' she said.

'He's not a medic, you silly cow!' snarled Spinx. He was sober and therefore in a filthy temper.

'Oh,' sniffed Queenie, 'I thought he was one of those phoney docs.'

'No, he's a brainy fella,' said Spinx, 'so lay off him.' He raised a hammy fist to Queenie's face but she never turned a hair. She just grimaced and nonchalantly filled up her glass of gin and tonic.

So that evening Joe was invited to the office for the first time. The office turned out to be a small attic right at the top of Queenie's Bar. Climbing the steep stairs, Joe passed a series of low-beamed attics, and he realised that this was a very old building and that the attics were part of an ancient dwelling. Small high windows gave magnificent views right down over the Thames, as they must have done for hundreds of years, and the ceilings sloped almost to the floor, except in the centre room which was larger. It was also furnished, with a bed, an old chair and an old-fashioned desk.

When Joe arrived, Spinx was presiding over some kind of meeting. Snatcher was there, lolling on the bed, as was Doug, who sat on a small chair. He was sitting astride it, back to front, his battered face on his hands, leaning on the back of the chair as he listened to Spinx. Behind the door, looking rather furtive, stood the Hustler. His arms were folded and for once he was wearing a clean white roll-neck jersey.

Joe felt rather breathless from the number of stairs he had just climbed and he hesitated at the door. A little flutter of fear ran through him, for he sensed that the committee had been discussing him.

'Come in, Joe,' roared Spinx. Joe stepped forward, and, in a silent, somewhat sinister manner, Hustler closed the door carefully behind him.

This is it, thought Joe, *death or honour* . . . He almost trembled in anticipation.

He was soon put out of his misery. 'We have voted you in, Joe,' said Spinx. 'You have met all the boys now,' he said. 'We are only a small organisation.' He sounded like the chairman of a board of directors. The whole procedure was carried out in this manner, stiff and formal, with no laughter or chatter. It was all very serious. Spinx explained their role to Joe and added, 'Since the Gaffer got nicked we have kept going and stayed out of trouble. I intend to keep it that way,' he added, narrowing his eyes and looking around challengingly as though expecting someone to dispute that statement.

'This is how I look at it,' he continued. 'Joe's a brainy bloke,' he said to his gang. 'He may not be much good out on the job but as an inside bloke, he's ideal.'

There were nods and grunts of assent from the boys.

'I know he's got form and we have to be careful 'cause if Old Bill knows he's around he will suss him out, that's for sure. But seeing that he got done for manslaughter, he probably won't be connected with the old safe blowers.' Spinx grinned and looked very pleased with himself.

Joe was really astounded by these words. It was as he had suspected all along. This lot knew all about Maisie. He felt angry but remained dumb.

The boss had made his opening speech so now it was the turn of the boys.

'Better get him a new Monica,' said Doug in his deep, husky voice.

'Good idea,' said Spinx. 'We all have a nickname,' he explained to Joe.

'What are we going to call him?' demanded Snatcher from his comfortable perch on the bed.

'What about Professor?' suggested Hustler.

'No, Stubby's got a bloke called that,' returned Spinx. 'We don't wanna get mixed up with them bastards.'

'Tell yer what, he looks like a yid with that big conk. Why don't we call him Yossel – that's Yiddish for Joe,' Snatcher informed them.

Joe was rather sensitive about his heavy Polish

features and put a protective hand over his nose. This gesture seemed to amuse the younger lads who went into fits of laughter.

But Spinx banged loudly on the desk. 'Order!' he shouted. They obediently stopped and silence was resumed once more.

'Now, Joe,' continued Spinx, eyeing Joe in a speculative manner, 'you've got to change your appearance. Grow your hair or your beard, and yer might get some different gear, like a pair of fancy pants and a bright shirt. You know the caper. You can kip up here, and they will give you grub from downstairs. If anyone asks who you are, you're called Yossel, and you're some foreigner here painting the river scene. Is that okay with you?'

Joe was amused. Having imposed a new name and identity on him, Spinx had the audacity to ask him if it was okay. He wanted to grin but he thought it wiser to restrain himself. 'I won't be a prisoner up here, I hope,' he said. 'I don't fancy being cooped up again. I've just got out.'

But Spinx slapped him violently on the back. 'No, you silly sod. There's the way out – down the fire escape there . . .' He opened the door and showed him a long twisted iron staircase that went right down to the banks of the river. 'Now, mate, go in and out here and paint yer bleeding head off if it suits yer. But remember don't go up no labour exchange or social security offices. If you run out of cash someone will bung yer, but above all, keep the old trap shut.' He put his finger to the side of his nose, meaning that Joe was not to talk under any circumstances. It was the best known sign in Stepney.

'You can all blow now,' said Spinx finally ending the meeting. 'I'll stay and help Yossel settle in. Bring up a bottle, will yer, lad?' he asked Hustler. 'And tell the Queen to send up some dinner.'

Looking a trifle depressed, the Hustler stood holding out his hand. 'Give me the money for the bottle, Guv, you know what Queenie's like . . .'

With a broad grin, Spinx produced a fiver. 'Here you are,' he said. 'Keep the change. We must not upset the Queen. Proper little business woman, is our Queenie. Don't know what we'd do without her.'

Joe was interested in the way these men all regarded Queenie. The boys showed great respect for her, as well as an element of fear, while the large jovial Spinx seemed almost contemptuous of her.

Ten minutes later, Hustler returned with a bundle of bed linen and a bottle of scotch which Spinx immediately set upon. He poured Joe a huge tumbler full and took one for himself. He finished it with a loud gulp. Joe took his glass and added water to it. He had no intention of risking a repeat of the fiasco the other night.

'That's it, we're all fixed up, Yossel,' declared the boss, raising his refilled glass. 'You'll find I'm not such a bad guv'nor, as long as you play straight with me.'

Joe looked into those blue granite eyes and suddenly got the curious sense of being fourteen again and being interviewed by his first employer. Perhaps there was still time to back out of all this, he thought, but it would not be easy.

'What will be my assignment?' he asked mildly.

'That's the spirit,' said Spinx with approval. 'Good, let's get to work.' From his light-coloured waistcoat with the line of pearly buttons, Spinx produced a crumpled piece of paper. Then he rummaged around in the desk and pulled out a small guide of the London streets. Joe watched as the large clean hands smoothed the pages, the huge knuckle-duster rings flashed, and the diamonds in the ring on his little finger glinted in the sun.

With a pencil and a large magnifying glass, Spinx drew a square around a small city area. 'See that, Joe? I want you to draw that area, but very big, on a large sheet of paper. I want every street and every corner marked out so it can all be clearly seen. Get the outline in and then we'll go down to get the rest of the details from sight.'

Joe stared at him. 'Why do you want the map, may I ask?' His voice was quiet, as he hoped that his question would not enrage the other man. Fortunately it did not.

'We'll pull a safe job every so often,' explained Spinx. 'Nothing too spectacular. We'll do it in a quiet way. We are not greedy, just careful. But the boys haven't had a lot of schooling. Even me, I never could learn from a book. But it's all up there . . .' He banged his head with his huge fist. 'The Gaffer was the one with the brains,' he continued, 'but then he got bleeding greedy and got himself nicked. So I want all the next ones planned. This time we can't afford mistakes. We got to be careful. Another dose of porridge might finish me, I know that. Can you do the map, Joe? What do you think?'

'Nothing to it,' Joe replied casually. 'I'll start today.'

'Good lad!' Spinx gave Joe a violent thump on the back. Then he looked at his expensive wristwatch. 'I've got to go. Me old lady don't like to be kept waiting. We're popping down the coast to visit my daughter. I've got two lovely grandsons,' he added proudly.

Joe was impressed by the complexity of Spinx's character and the different character he revealed to different people; whether the hard-faced boss, the willing husband or the devoted grandad. It was rather touching.

When the boss had left, Joe climbed into the narrow

bed and slept soundly until sunrise. When he opened his eyes, he looked around at the black and white contrast between the grimy walls and the low oak beams. Momentarily, he wondered where he was. He went to the window and looked down at the river, the deep dark river. It was very pleasant up here, he thought. What a wonderful studio it would make.

As Joe breathed in the clear air, ideas came pouring in, ideas for turning his new abode into a magnificent studio. And the small room off it would be perfect for paint mixing and could even serve as a dark room. The other little room off to the right would make a good kitchen. In this room he decided he would paint a brightly coloured mural over the whole wall.

As Joe unfolded the laundered sheets and made up the narrow bed by the wall, he imagined his easel and canvas positioned by the window and the moonlit river scene emerging upon it, slowly forming as he worked. He placed his shaving gear on the shelf. He felt as though he were in a dream. Was he really now part of a criminal gang? He smiled to himself. 'Why worry, Joe?' he muttered. 'What have you got to be so concerned about? You're already on the wrong side of the law and so who's going to care?' He tidied up the bed and hung his other clean shirt on a hanger. Then he stood back to survey the room. It looked quite cosy. Joe broke into laughter. 'Why, you've come home, Joe,' he chuckled, 'and it's better than underneath the arches with the rest of the down-and-outs.'

The first week of inactivity passed peacefully by. At night Joe would sit by the window watching the sun go down. Patches of dark cloud, like black stallions, rode into the red fire of the sun. Then slowly the mist came riding up strongly, twisting high in between the lofty wharves. At high tide little tugs churned down through the water and large steamers hooted and tooted outside the bridge. Joe was feeling very anxious to paint it all. He had to buy some artist's paints and an easel. He was broke, but he might come by some easy money, he thought, and, according to the boys, that should be very soon.

Every evening as the darkness came, Joe lay on the narrow bed and looked around his new home. At this time of day, it looked eerie. The naked white glare from the one electric bulb cast long shadows around the low ceiling. In the dark corners odd shapes seemed to lurk, and a large black stain in the middle of the floorboards gave him the creeps. What a strange place it was. He felt as though he were in limbo, waiting and waiting for something to happen. And he wondered how many other lodgers this attic had harboured before him.

Chapter Nine

The Old Firm

Joe worked very hard drawing the map to scale on a huge piece of drawing paper. The area concerned was small, just that bit of land between Cannon Street Station and Tower Bridge.

During the day, Joe was engaged in his task and no one bothered him. At meal times he went down to the kitchen to eat with the staff who either ignored him or entertained him, depending on their mood or the amount of work that had to be got through.

The place was always busy. In one bar city workers came in for lunch and drinks, the boys hung around playing darts, while in another smaller bar old women sat squeezed in rows where they consumed large amounts of beer and sandwiches and gossiped. They were often joined by Fat Lot, who turned down the sandwiches, preferring a liquid lunch instead, in the company of her old cronies. Joe always lunched with sweet Nelly, while Queenie, perched high on her stool, of course, chatted to the bank managers and shipping clerks who frequented her establishment. Her poker face and stilted movements remained the same, as her quick brain gathered every useful bit of information she heard, absorbing it for future reference, just like a bright-eyed squirrel stores her nuts for hibernation. Joe often felt left out of the conversations around him because he could not understand what was being said. He had to turn to the chirpy Nelly to translate for him.

'Nelly,' he asked rather apologetically one day, 'what does "bung yer" mean? Spinx said Queenie would bung me so long as she gets it back . . .'

Nelly stared at him for a moment and then went off into peals of high-pitched giggles. On regaining her breath she explained. 'It's slang,' she said. 'It just means that Queenie will give you some money.'

Joe sighed. 'It's all foreign to me,' he said. 'It's a complete language of its own. Give me the lowdown on it, Nelly. What are the rules of cockney slang?'

'Well,' said Nelly, ticking off the various quotations on her stubby fingers, 'there's "apples and pears", that means stairs; there's "whistle and flute", that means suit; there's "teapot lids" for kids . . .' She then rattled off a whole list of them.

Joe was amused and delighted. 'That will do me for now,' he said. 'I must absorb today's lesson. Thank you, Nelly. Ha, to think that it's from this small island that the real King's English originated.'

Nelly disregarded this last remark, for it had no meaning for her. But she had warmed to her subject and chatted on in her cockney accent.

Not wishing to miss any more, Joe reached for his little notebook and began to write down each expression as it came out of Nelly's mouth. It was a marvellously lively language, enriched and kept alive by Jewish expressions brought to London by the thousands of immigrants who had flocked to the East End in the past century to escape persecution elsewhere, such as the Jews escaping pogroms in Russia and Poland. And, of course, many home-coming sailors had also brought back new words and sayings from other parts of the world. And so in this little book, Joe began a dossier on Queenie's Bar and its environment.

After lunch, as Joe was finishing his tea, Queenie came up and threw a twenty-pound note on the table.

Joe looked shocked. Did she expect something from him in return?

'Here, it's only a loan,' said Queenie, ignoring his expression, 'and let Nelly go with you. Go down to Solly's to get some gear. Tell Solly to send me the bill.'

Joe was confused by these instructions but he picked up the note as Queenie sauntered off without waiting for any thanks or appreciation.

Nelly was ready to leave straight away. 'Come on, Joe,' she urged, 'I've got to get the kids from school. Hurry up!' Joe was hustled out into the cool street with its tall warehouses which blocked out much of the light. Because of the warehouses, Stern Street had a gloomy sort of atmosphere but the little rows of houses on each side of the street still looked spick and span. Every knocker and door handle shone like glass, the doorsteps were scrubbed white and the lace curtains inside the windows were spotless.

'This is our street, Joe,' Nelly told him. 'That's my house, there, number eight. Been there since I was a kid. It used to be me muvver's house, and now they're going to pull it down. I don't want to live in the high flats, but it will be nice to have a bathroom.' Nelly chattered gaily as she walked beside Joe, glancing up every now and then at his face. They made a funny pair, her five foot height to his six.

They went down the end of the row where a grimy shop stood on a corner. Three dirty brass balls hung outside overhead and the window was full of an untidy display of secondhand clothes.

'Used to be the old pawn shop, this did,' explained

Nelly. 'Don't know what our mum would have done without old Solly in those good old days. But it's all different now. He's got some good gear in the back now – it's all knocked off, but who cares?' She giggled like a young girl.

They entered the dim interior of the shop and were served by an elderly old man who gesticulated a lot but said little. From the back of the premises he brought out some beautiful shirts which would have proudly graced any counter in Carnaby Street. Joe watched him with interest. Old Solly looked secretive, and throughout the transaction he kept a furtive eye on the door. No one needed to be told that this was not honestly acquired merchandise.

As Joe considered the clothes and tried to decide what to buy, Nelly went off to collect her children from school. Joe selected some flowery shirts and some corduroy trousers, two flowery cravats and a black beret.

Solly wrapped the goods, muttering and mumbling all the time that business was very bad. He nodded when Joe told him to send the bill to Queenie and grunted when Joe left and said goodbye.

Half-way down the small street Joe noticed an opening. There were two high wooden gates with the words 'Builders and Decorators' written up on them. Below the sign stood a small, middle-aged man who was dressed in a youthful manner in a short white-belted mackintosh. His bushy white hair stood up like a wire mop, and his long sideburns were carefully clipped. If he had been a woman he would have been described as mutton dressed up as lamb. His small eyes peered at Joe through steel-rimmed spectacles.

Joe looked at him with amusement and wished that he had a sketch-book with him. Then he realised that the small man was beckoning to him in a very mysterious manner. Joe hesitated. He did not want to pass by him. But the man soon spoke to him. His voice was high pitched. 'In here, Yossel,' he said. 'I'll show you the back way to Queenie's.'

At last the penny dropped. This odd creature was stationed here specifically to guide him to the back entrance of Queenie's Bar. It was too risky to go through the bar with his new gear. Joe smiled. How well-tuned they all were, and how wary. Each one was like a small but important cog in a big criminal wheel. It was quite fascinating. Joe was beginning to feel a certain admiration for all these people. In a way it was so basic, so primitive, a return to the time when each chief guarded his clan and each caveman his own cave.

Cut into one of the high gates was a small door which the little man now opened very quietly, and bent down to go inside. Joe followed him. Now he found himself in an alley-way in which several old, battered cars were lying around. Further along there was a small garage where the blue flash of welding equipment came through a crack in the door as they passed. They walked on and then clambered over a boulder surrounded by brick and rubble. Once more they were beside the river. A slipway went down into the murky water and beside it, standing stark on the skyline, Joe could now see Queenie's. For the first time he noticed that on one side of the weather vane there was a ship, and on the north side there was a miniature castle.

He stared up at it. 'Is that really a castle up on the weather vane?' he asked his guide.

'Yes,' replied the man. 'This place used to be called the Ship and Castle but mostly it's known as the Ship now . . . except by our locals,' he added, 'and we call it Queenie's Castle. It's very old, this place,' he went on. 'Some say it goes back to the sixteen hundreds.

At one time it used to be the haunt of smugglers and pirates, but of course it's all been modernised since then.' He chuckled at his little joke.

Joe did not reply. He found the whole place intriguing.

'I'm Hustler's Pop,' the little man was telling him. 'Now, that's the way up the fire escape. You can go in and out, and not be seen. And no one gets past that gate we went through, not while I'm around they don't.' He puffed out his small chest in a boastful manner, and Joe was reminded of a little robin redbreast with feathers all puffed aggressively defending his nest.

'Who the devil is Hustler's Pop?' Joe asked Nelly the next day.

'Oh, he's Hustler's old man, or supposed to be,' Nelly replied as she swiftly peeled potatoes.

'What do you mean?' he asked, picking up a knife to help her. He was learning just how to dig information from Nelly.

'Well,' declared Nelly. 'Hustler's the other way.' She lowered her voice as though imparting some dark secret.

'Other way?' Joe gazed helplessly at her.

'Oh, you know,' Nelly giggled bashfully and gave him a nudge with her elbow.

Joe now understood. 'Is he now?' He grinned in embarrassment.

'Well,' continued Nelly, 'that horrible little man who calls himself his pop, ain't really his farver.' She resumed her gossipy manner, washing the skinned potatoes vigorously under the tap. 'Hustler's Pop took him in when Hustler was a kid escaping from an approved school. And there's plenty of people who think that it was him that turned Hustler the other way. Dirty old sod,' Nelly sniffed.

'It's not my cup of tea, Nelly,' said Joe with a twinkle, 'but, of course, if *you* fancy me . . .'

'Pack it up, Joe,' said Nelly giving him a push. 'Now, I've got to get this dinner on.' Her manner was brisk but her blushes betrayed her. 'Fancy yourself because you got some new gear on?' was her last caustic comment as he went off to his rooms.

Joe smiled. Nelly was a fiery old thing and he liked her.

Queenie's Castle was always full of surprises. The Queen herself suddenly came into the kitchen with her coffee after lunch. She seated herself down to face Joe. Her little bright eyes flickered over his new shirt, then down his corduroy pants.

'Nice bit of gear, that, Joe,' she said in a pleasant cajoling tone which sent a shiver up his spine. As Queenie leaned over the scent of violets wafted up his nostrils. The soft blonde hair almost brushed his face. She finished her coffee, picked her teeth, and flashed a bright smile at him. 'Fancy a bit of the other, Joe?' she asked sweetly. It was almost as though she were asking the time of day.

Joe froze. A quivering sensation rose up in him but he dropped his eyes and shook his head. He had to resist. 'No thanks, Queenie,' he said politely, 'I'm going to be busy this afternoon.' He then waited in breathless suspense for the response to this snub. But Queenie just rose casually to her feet, stretched and yawned.

'It's all right, Joe, I'll ask old Bulldog. He's always ready to oblige!' In an upright and stately manner, she sauntered away. Joe heard her make a quick phone call before going upstairs for her afternoon siesta.

Joe looked at Nelly and he could tell by the expression on her face that she had overheard that short conversation. 'Who the devil is old Bulldog?' he whispered. He was feeling quite shocked.

Nelly giggled. 'He's a guard sergeant stationed at the Tower. We all call him Bulldog because he looks like one.'

Joe shook his head. 'What a licentious little bitch!' he muttered. He felt churned up inside, regretful that he had not accepted the invitation into Queenie's bed but determined not to be used by her whenever she chose.

'Oh, don't be so hard on her,' Nelly defended her mistress. 'She's not so bad, she just can't help it. I've known her since she was a kid working in the strip joints, and some people need it more than others. A bit of nooky is like a drug to her, a fix, you might say.'

Joe was not sure if he had had a lucky escape or missed an opportunity. But he was confused. For the next few days he decided to avoid Queenie, so he spent most of the day on Tower Hill making quick sketches of the beefeaters, the stone tower and the visiting tourists. They were clever sketches which vividly portrayed this historic city in the late 1960's, and they kept Joe happy.

They say that listeners never hear good of themselves and this was true for Joe. One morning, while he was shaving, he overheard a conversation between Fat Lot and Hustler's Pop who were in the office.

'It's always the same with these clever blokes,' It was the high-pitched voice of Hustler's Pop. 'These artists and writers, bums, the whole bloody lot of them! They just can't help it.'

Joe froze. His face was half covered with lather. Were they talking about him? Surely not.

'Seems a nice enough fellow to me,' continued Hustler's Pop. 'Pity he got mixed up with the missus. He'll get a knife in his guts for sure if Gaffer gets out.'

So it *was* him they were discussing, and that was what they really thought of him – a bum. Joe felt very hurt. But it was interesting that they all seemed as scared of this mysterious Gaffer just as John had been . . .

The next day Joe met Queenie in the small dark passageway that led to the bar. Without thinking, he placed his hands on the wall as if to prevent her passing.

Queenie stared at him and for a fleeting second a glint of amusement came into those deep-set eyes. But then they hardened again and her lips clamped down in that hard line. 'Excuse me, Joe,' she said. 'I'm very busy now.'

But Joe remained in position and waved the packet of notes he had in his hand. 'I owe you some money, I'd like to repay it,' he said. That quivering sensation had risen up inside him again. And no one was to call him a bum or a ponce.

Queenie took the notes and stuffed them down her cleavage in a most professional manner. 'Ta, Joe, never say no to a nice bit of lolly,' she said brightly. Then ducking swiftly under his arm, she returned to her throne, that seat beside the counter where she sat with her regal air, alert and attentive to every move that went on about her.

Despondency crept through Joe's veins. What was the right way to chip the ice from that frosty barrier except in bed?

Chapter Ten

The Waterfront

Joe had finished reproducing the map and he spent most of the next few days sitting on the river wall. He loved to watch the peaceful old Father Thames flowing relentlessly down to the sea. Life on the river was varied and interesting, and the bright summer sun made the old warehouses glow with previously hidden colour. With his sketch-book on his knees, Joe began to feel quite relaxed. This way of life was quite pleasing to him.

Hustler's Pop often visited him on his way to have a 'wet', which was, Joe discovered, a glass of beer. They were frequently joined by a burly young man named Pickles who worked in the small garage workshop in the alley. He liked being in Joe's pictures, too. He often joined Joe at the waterside. Clad in greasy overalls, his red hair almost unrecognisable under its cloak of grease, he would insist on being sketched with his back to the river scene. 'There's no place like the old smokey river, mate,' he told Joe. 'I was in the merchant navy. Seen all the world, I have,' he announced proudly, 'but the sight of the old Thames roaring under the bridge still always thrills me.'

Joe swiftly outlined the wide grinning face, the greasy mop of hair and crumpled blue overalls.

Pickles was a lively, charming lad and was always very pleased with his portraits.

One day Hustler's Pop was busy elsewhere and Joe and Pickles had a drink on their own. Pickles went to the bar and brought back two foaming pints of beer. The two men sat on the wall and had a long conversation. Joe looked at the thick thighs and muscular arms of this lad; he had the magnificent physique of an athlete. He could be a champion wrestler. More than six feet in height, he seemed wasted in that back-street garage.

'Is that your own business?' Joe asked.

Pickles shook his head. 'No, mate, I'm on the firm. Didn't you know?' He was surprised at Joe's ignorance.

Joe felt strangely disappointed. Here was another man tied down to the firm. But then who was he to talk? He himself would not be here if he were not also tied up some way with this criminal circle.

Pickles chatted on. 'Good with engines, I am. I bodge up all the hot cars.' Pickles finished his beer, put his leg over the wall to sit astride it, and stared ruefully down the river. 'I always get this same feeling when I'm down here,' he said. 'I want to get up, jump a bloody ship and sail away.'

'Well, so why don't you?' suggested Joe.

'I can't,' replied the lad gloomily. 'I'm in too deep.'

Joe had begun to sketch the outlines of Tower Bridge. His pencil moved slowly and carefully. Pausing for a moment, he looked up and saw the sadness on the youth's full face and the expression you might see on a trapped animal.

It lasted just a second. Pickles suddenly swung his sturdy leg back over the wall. 'Better get some work done. So long, Yossel.'

Joe looked back at the water rushing past and

thought how much like the river his current life was. It was full of charming people such as Nelly and Pickles, so varied and fun, but always in the background there was an element of danger. It was just like the Thames, so clear and full midstream but dark, oily and polluted in the shallows.

One evening Joe was finishing a landscape painting he had been working on all day. He would always remember the excitement he felt that day as the sun went down, fighting against time in the evening shadows. The sky was absolutely scarlet. Never before had Joe observed such a magnificent exit of that lordly sun as it stayed trembling in a kind of black-and-gold fiery land. The wind had risen and black storm clouds swept past like a herd of stallions riding into the red fire. Down on earth the dark river picked up the colours of the sky and jumbled them rainbow-like in the deep water. The outgoing tide rapidly took the red, purple, blue and green tones along with it until, losing out to the nightfall, the sun disappeared, leaving Tower Bridge looking like a fairytale castle with its tall towers. A few glints of light shone a silver blue on the ship's funnels anchored below.

Swiftly and expertly, as the lovely vision passed through his eye to his brain, Joe transferred it onto the canvas to reveal a scene of astounding beauty. Feeling very happy and perfectly relaxed, Joe put away his paints and brushes and admired his handiwork. He was feeling so immensely satisfied and self-absorbed that when Hustler's Pop approached him across the paved yard, he was not aware of him until he heard the high-pitched voice.

'Well, that's really a wonderful job, Yossel. You're a lucky fellow to be able to paint like that. I'm going for a drink. You want to come with me around the public? It's nice and quiet around there.'

'I'll take the gear up and then I'll join you,' replied Joe. 'Where did you say you were going?'

'Around the backs,' replied Hustler's Pop, pointing down the alley-way. 'At the Jug and Bottle. There's a little door down there.' With that he tripped away on his tiny feet with polished shoes that shone like glass.

Chapter Eleven

The Jug and Bottle

The discovery of the Jug and Bottle bar was something of an adventure. Joe made his way down the alley-way and pushed open that frosted glass door. Feeling timorous, he entered the bar.

Red velvet hangings shut off the public bar from the ostentatious lounge bar next door. The public bar was long and narrow with plain unvarnished panelled walls. There were no fancy fittings in the public bar, and long wooden benches lined the walls. The well-scrubbed wooden floorboards were sprinkled with sawdust and there was a distinct odour of stale human sweat combined with strong ale.

The counter was furnished with large old-fashioned brass beer pumps over which presided none other than Beery Bill. Looking around, Joe immediately recognised Fat Lot sitting amongst the men and women on the long bench. Her large shape seemed to take up most of the room. She was clad in her best clothes, a black silk dress and an artificial pearl choker. Her cheeks were red and rosy and her eyes sparkled quite fiercely. Overall, she was quite an impressive sight.

Around her sat several old people. There a little lady in a battered straw hat, two bewhiskered old men and one old codger who stared out from unseeing eyes. In his arthritic hands he clutched a white walking stick.

Hustler's Pop had settled himself by the counter and seemed to be buying drinks all round. The other customers waited for their drinks in a mouth-watering line, their cracked old lips twitching. Pop was in the money and it was going to be an exceptionally good drinking night.

'Come in, Yossel!' Pop called. Joe walked over and took a seat facing the old women and men. He felt quite sad as he looked at them all. In this bar they congregated, the old and the disabled, the dregs of the small street. The bar provided a kind of haven after years of stormy seas.

But Joe soon discovered that there was no need to feel pity, for the faster the beer flowed the livelier the conversation became. The discussion went from gee gees to football, from politics to war. It was lively, carefree and invigorating. A young lad came over to ask Joe to join the darts match. Joe was willing to have a go but he found that he was not too good at this skilled game which they all took so seriously. But the other lads were amicable and had fun in their own way. They laughed at his mistakes, banged him hard on the back and loaded him with pints of beer.

By now the oldies had begun to sing along with the music from an old piano standing in the corner which was played by a white-haired old lady whose delicate hands caressed the keys like white butterflies. And Joe, having presented Beery Bill with five pounds to buy drinks for everyone, found that he was the most popular man in the bar. The firm, Queenie and all those soul-destroying weeks of indecision were temporarily forgotten. Everyone was happy, laughing and singing, and they all joined in the old variety songs, listening to solo numbers and singing in a real cockney dialect. Somebody went out to buy fish and chips which he ate with his hands. He enjoyed it as much as the rest of the company, especially since it was accompanied by the sound of Hustler's Pop singing. He did not have a bad voice, either.

After a few hours, Hustler's Pop came up to him. 'Come on, Joe,' he said. 'Come home with me, we're going to have a ding-dong.'

Joe was feeling very drunk, almost as drunk as the two old ladies who left the pub swaying from side to side and carrying a crate of beer between them as they disappeared down the street. Joe breathed in deep to get the night air into his lungs. Standing still he propped himself against the wall, wishing that his legs did not feel so wobbly. Where was Hustler's Pop? There was no one to guide him. He was trying to remember which way to turn in order to find the iron fire escape that led to his roof-top home, when from an adjoining doorway a blonde head appeared. It was Queenie about to bolt the door of her castle.

'Are you coming in, Joe, or staying out there all night?' Her voice was warm and inviting.

Joe opened his mouth to talk but no words came out. He just put out a long arm and took the outstretched hand.

'Oh, come on, love,' she cooed. 'Fancy leaving you as drunk as this.' The blonde head came close, smelling so sweet and feeling so soft. Then a strong young shoulder held him upright, as Queenie guided him inside.

Inside the dark hall, Joe's arms went about her firm body, fumbling clumsily around her waist.

'It's all right, Joe,' she whispered, placing her arms about his neck and pressing close to him. 'Come on,' she said urgently. 'Let's go to bed . . .'

Joe's was a hazy memory but something wonderful happened that night in Queenie's bed. His experience with women was fairly limited. His wife Mary in

America had been cold and timid, Anne loving but very respectable. But the Queen was something different. She was a real woman with powerful animal passions. What she did to him and what she asked him to do to her were things he had never even imagined . . .

Some time later Joe slowly opened heavy eyelids which were barely able to function. He looked about him. It was morning and the strong light of day hurt his eyes. He looked around at the unfamiliar flowered patterns on the wallpaper and the lavender silk drapes. Where on earth was he?

Turning to his side he saw Queenie, cuddled up between the sheets like a kitten. He looked down at her small finely chiselled face, and noticed that black streaks of mascara had run down her cheeks. He put his finger softly on her face. The skin was still wet where she had cried in her sleep.

Joe was touched to know that she had feelings, this hard-faced strumpet from whom he had found it so difficult to free himself. Tenderly, he tucked the sheet about her to cover up those well-formed naked limbs. A mental image flashed through his brain of her lovemaking the night before. She had used her lips and her hands like sweet, passionate aids to make a man feel that life was ecstasy. Certainly Joe felt that he had never experienced this before now.

The gentle smile on his face disappeared as he suddenly thought of the other men who had lain with Queenie – the Bulldog and a succession of long-haired youths. He winced as a tight feeling of disgust clutched at his throat. He had a strong urge to grab that slim neck and throttle the life from it, but instead he ran from the room.

Chapter Twelve

The First Job

At last the big day dawned. Although life had been quite dreary for Joe, the other lads had in fact been very busy working out the details of the big job they were planning.

It was unusually quiet in the lounge bar at lunch-time. The wide boys were all conspicuous by their absence. The Queen sat perched high on her throne as neat and precise as ever. She wore a slick, tight, black roll-necked sweater and white satin slacks, and she graciously entertained her lunch-time customers, mostly white-collar workers from the surrounding office blocks.

Nelly was busy in the kitchen but she was very depressed today. Her face was pale and her eyes were red with weeping. Over lunch she confided to Joe the extent of her troubles: her two sons had been picked up by the police and Nelly was heartbroken.

'I've tried to be so careful with them, Joe,' she wept.

'Little boys are not criminals, Nelly,' Joe consoled her. 'They will soon send them home again.'

'But they will end up bad, Joe, because that's how it all starts,' Nelly sobbed.

'Nonsense, they will only be warned not to do it again,' he told her.

But Nelly was convinced she was right. 'I've seen it all my life, Joe. The bloody cops just hound the kids into crime. It was the same with my own brothers. Just because our old man was inside, bloody jail bait we all were down here,' she declared.

'There certainly doesn't seem to be any place for them to play and occupy themselves,' said Joe. 'What did they do?'

'They took a bit of lead wire from a derelict house, that's all. They all go the same way,' she continued mournfully, 'approved school, Borstal, and then Parkhurst.'

Joe felt very distressed to see the cheery Nelly so unhappy and he did his best to comfort her. He was interested in her comments as there was a certain truth to them. Prison certainly seemed to be no deterrent to these East-Enders. It was absurd. There had to be something lacking in a social system that bred whole families of criminals from generation to generation. Starting with petty pilfering, these lads progressed to worse crimes. Attitudes were inherited, passed down from father to son. And who was responsible? It was awfully hard to disentangle the reasons – lack of parental discipline, ever-zealous police, lack of ambition, something led to these young men going astray and being shut up like cattle in a shed for the best part of their lives. What was the answer to it all?

Joe sat pondering the social ills of the modern world and then began to think of his own parents. They had been immigrants from Poland, coming to a strange land during the Depression when money was so hard to come by. Night and day they had worked hard, and they always worked hard enough so that money could be found for music lessons and educational books. He wondered what they would think of their bright boy now, who was slowly becoming an habitual criminal.

He pressed his cigarette into the ashtray with a sigh of deep nervous tension. From her perch, Queenie shot him a malevolent glare, and he knew it was time for him to return upstairs where he had been ordered to stay near the phone.

Reluctantly he climbed the three flights of stairs to his attic apartment and lay on the bed while the day ticked slowly by.

At ten o'clock Queenie came up bringing a bottle of whisky for the boss. 'Stay awake, Joe,' she snapped in a business-like manner. 'All being well, they'll be back by midnight.' It was as if their lovemaking had never happened.

At midnight, there was scarcely a sound in the attic but the kitchen tap dripped slowly and monotonously until every splish splash sounded like the crash of cymbals, so tense were Joe's nerves.

He drew the mouldy black-out curtains over the window. They were grim relics of the Blitz, so many years before. The boss had told him not to leave the light on late. 'You can spot this place a mile down river,' he had said.

But now the atmosphere in the attic seemed very close and still. It was also rather creepy. Grim ghosts of the past stalked the room as Joe lay tossing on his bed, endlessly waiting and wondering what the next hours would bring. He lit cigarette after cigarette. At times he drifted into sleep and hazy nightmares tried to overwhelm him. The voice of the unfortunate Maisie came though, high pitched and giggling, and then he heard another hoarse whisper, 'Do the dirty bleeder!' Half-asleep, it felt to Joe as if a heavy fist crashed into his face.

Forcing himself to wake, he hoisted himself quickly from the bed and began to pace the floor. Oh God, this was agony. How had he managed to get into such a predicament? He glanced at his watch. It was well past midnight. It was now ten minutes to three. Something must have gone wrong . . .

Just as he was about to panic, the door rattled and a shadowy form showed throughout the glass panel. Joe held his breath and then a voice called, 'Open up, Yossel!' It was Snatcher – first back from the scene of the crime. He pushed past Joe looking hot, tired and dusty but he was grinning jubilantly. 'It's over, Yos, and we had it away.' He plonked himself down on the bed. 'Pour me a drink, mate,' he asked. 'Doug won't be long, he's in the bog.'

Joe looked at Snatcher in astonishment. It seemed amazing to him that after all the stress and mental pressure that he had endured that evening, all these men could think about was having a drink or empty-ing their bowels. Without a word, he opened the whisky Queenie had brought up earlier and passed it to Snatcher.

Moments later they heard soft footsteps coming up the fire escape and then Doug appeared puffing like a billy goat. He looked very peculiar, almost headless with a nylon stocking stretched over his battered features. 'Oh, Gawd, ain't it funny? It always makes me want to shit,' he laughed as he pulled off his nylon mask.

'No, it ain't funny,' retorted Snatcher, downing his drink in one gulp. 'There was me travelling at sixty trying to dodge Old Bill and you breaking wind and making a nasty stink.' Then he smiled and they both laughed.

Joe poured them both a drink, and they casually discussed how easy their night's work had been. 'The boss won't be back until the morning, Joe,' said Snatcher, 'we might as well all get some kip.' He turned over on the bed as Doug retied the laces in the old plimsolls he wore.

'I'm going home,' said Doug. 'See you tomorrow.' And off he went.

Joe spent the rest of the night in an armchair unable to sleep. He felt rather confused. He had not been sure what to expect but certainly nothing as casual as this. What an anticlimax.

Nothing very spectacular happened in the morning either. Queenie pottered leisurely about the bar and Nelly cooked the lunch, her face hot and flushed beside the oven as she basted a huge joint of beef. 'I like to get the fat over it,' Nelly announced in her chatty manner.

To while away the time, Joe peeled potatoes and cut up lumps of cabbage, tossing them into a large pot on the stove. Upstairs Snatcher still slept. So far no one had even mentioned the goings-on of the previous night. Nelly certainly did not. She just chattered on endlessly about her forthcoming visit to her husband in prison. 'I don't know what he's going to say about the boys getting into bother,' she said, banging pots and pans about the kitchen.

'Then why enlighten him?' asked Joe.

Nelly stared at him askance. 'Not tell him?' cried Nelly. 'Why, the kids tell him everything, he makes them.' She closed the oven door with a defiant slam.

There seemed to be an undercurrent of tension like an unexploded bomb on the premises. Spinx arrived at lunchtime and stood drinking among the city workers. Queenie looked a shade paler than usual but her beady eyes roamed the bar as alert and watchful as a cat. When two men later sauntered in wearing belted raincoats and cloth caps, with a nonchalant shrug of her shoulders, Queenie engaged them in a long conversation.

'Old Bill's in the bar,' warned Nelly.

Joe's heart missed a beat. This was it. He was about to be hauled back to prison.

But Nelly smiled. 'It's all okay,' she said. 'You would have got the signal if the lid came off.' He did not know exactly what she had meant but he got the gist of it anyway. This underworld jargon still confused Joe. The succulent roast beef almost stuck in his gut when he tried to eat his lunch, he was too nervous even to swallow. Yet no one else seemed worried.

The policemen left and business went on as before. After lunch, Joe was told to present himself to Spinx in the office. He climbed the stairs two at a time, so anxious was he to get this business over.

All the lads were there squatting on the floor or leaning against the wall. There was a granite-faced Spinx, and Snatcher with a hairy unshaven chin. Spud, a wiry little man with bushy eyebrows, was also there, along with Hustler's Pop and Pickles.

'Ah, Joe's here,' said Spinx rising slowly. 'Now to work.' Unlocking the desk, he took out a brown suitcase and threw back the lid. The case was stuffed full with bank notes.

Joe's jaw dropped in astonishment.

'Don't look so surprised, Yossel,' joked Spinx. 'That's our pay-off. We can't afford to lose it, that's why we have a guard up here. Now, me lad, get the ledger out and write it all down. No good at book work, I ain't, and we don't pay our lads in hot money. Now, four hundred smackers for Doug . . .' He aimed a bundle of notes at Doug. 'Then the same for Hustler and Spud. Snatcher gets fifty less 'cos I paid his bleeding maintenance money, I did.'

'Lay off the women,' he growled as Snatcher deftly caught his notes. 'Now, the same for Pickles,' continued Spinx, 'but five for the Queen seeing as she keeps the coppers happy. Now, there's five for me, who gets rid of the hot lolly, then three for you, Joe, and Hustler's Pop. The inside men get a bit less. Right? Get it all down, Joe, then pass the book around and let them all have a decker. I like to run the firm legit. Don't want no falling out over money, you know.'

Once the suitcase was empty, Spinx snapped it shut and handed it to Spud. 'Now you, get off, Spud. The boat's in this slip-way. I'll hang on until you're up-river.' He turned to the others. 'Now, piss off all of you and don't spend the lolly too quickly. Old Bill's always on the look-out for mugs.'

The gang began to disperse, some down the stairs, some down the fire escape. Then Joe heard the chug chug of a boat departing and the swift whine of a fast car.

Spinx drank several whiskies in quick succession. 'Pick up your loot, Joe,' he joked, 'or someone might nick it.'

A strange thrill went through Joe as his long sensitive fingers flicked back the notes. How easily he had earned his share and best of all, he did not regret it, he felt no remorse.

'Don't worry about it, Joe,' said Spinx as he breezed out. 'It's all good money.'

'I don't think I will worry,' murmured Joe, staring in wonder at the notes in his hand.

Once alone, Joe found himself looking apprehensively at the black patch on the floor. His mood changed. Other stooges like himself had passed this way, he was sure of that. He was now in as deep as he could be, and that bundle of notes seemed to be burning a hole in his back pocket. He felt that there was no doubt that the affable boy Snatcher could run him down in his car without a qualm. He shivered at the thought of that long stiletto which Hustler assiduously used to manicure his nails.

Joe heaved a deep sigh. *Well, if you can't beat 'em,*

join 'em, he thought. He walked across the room and washed under the cold dripping tap. He examined his face in the cracked mirror. He had not shaved for days and his hair had grown rather long. He was looking quite wild and woolly. He stuck his beret on his head at a jaunty angle and decided that it suited him best with the bright shirt and corduroy trousers. Now he really looked the part, whether as a travelling artist, an American tourist or even a hippy drop-out. But certainly no one would ever recognise that staid old teacher, Joe Walowski.

Taking fifty pounds from his pile of ill-gotten gains, Joe then stowed the rest away and sauntered out into the fresh air.

Half-way down the street, he spotted the tiny neat shape of Hustler's Pop furtively rolling a fag and looking from side to side.

'Going shopping, Joe?' he asked with sardonic humour.

'There's a good market just down the road,' he chuckled.

Joe rather liked that market. He had often hung about watching the stalls being set up, taking in the shouting bustling humour of its inhabitants. He loved to see the fruit being laid in neat rows, bright yellow bunches of bananas hanging amid dusty purple grapes. There was the Jewish lad who sang so well as he unloaded his wares of bright exotic materials, and the elderly couple who squabbled incessantly as they arranged a stall full of second-hand clothes. The market offered a brimful of a lusty bustly life, a patch of real living. Joe always felt that he wanted to capture it, to write about it, or paint it, he was not quite sure which.

As Joe walked along the market, he saw a small shop with paintings in the window. He had never noticed it before, so now he wandered in. The owner of the shop wore blue glasses, obscuring red, inflamed eyes. One half of the shop was a showroom for antiques while the other half displayed artist's materials. Joe spent a very rewarding hour talking with the owner about art and the pictures on display, and then gave him a big order for equipment and materials. After Joe had made his purchase, the owner was particularly friendly. He told Joe that before starting up this shop, he had drawn chalk pictures on the pavement in the West End. He was, he told Joe, struggling to survive in what was an unprofitable business.

As Joe left the shop, it occurred to him that that man was the only truly honest man he had come across for years, and certainly since living in the East End. So he was proof that they did exist, and Joe was glad of that.

Joe carried his easel, canvas and store of paints the full length of the market, watching the girls with their hair in rollers pushing toddlers in pushchairs, and the wide old women with huge shopping bags brimming over with food to be consumed by their families in the tall melancholy blocks of flats that looked down over the market.

Joe looked up at the long row of balconies with the lines of washing blowing in the breeze, and the windows, rows of them like sightless eyes. He breathed deeply and found himself smiling. How good it was to have money! Yes, he thought, he wanted to stay put in this grimy old carefree part of the big city. It had character and life.

When Joe got back to the bar, Queenie seemed unusually preoccupied. She informed him coldly that lunch would not be served that day owing to the absence of Nelly who had gone on a day trip to visit her husband. But Joe could take a beer and sandwich upstairs with him, if he wanted to, she told him.

Joe stared at her keenly. She seemed off-hand and did not smile. Beside her lolled her ardent pursuer, Bulldog. His thick arms resting on the counter were almost bursting out of the rough tweed jacket he wore, so big and muscular was his body. Looking at him, Joe could see why he was called Bulldog. He had wide flaring nostrils and protruding eyes, his cheeks had a purple tinge and his large nose was like a red pin-cushion full of tiny holes. What an unattractive hunk of human he was!

Joe nodded and retired to his lonely attic with a drink and some bread and cheese. He missed Nelly's warm chatter and companionship.

After he had eaten, he settled down to work. First he did a preliminary sketch of the graceful stretch of bridge and the little speed boats cutting across the murky waters, past the cargo vessel anchored nearby. When he had finished, he went down to the river wall, placed his easel in position and painted the Thames river scene, one of the many for his collection which would make his work famous in years to come.

Chapter Thirteen

A Happy Home

That evening Joe decided to treat himself to dinner at a little French restaurant in town where he and Anne used to eat. He settled into his seat and took in the same cool dark interior, the same soft-footed waiters, the excellent food and variety of wines. The restaurant was the same but he did not feel at ease there. He felt strange and lonely. Not even the head waiter recognised him. Wondering about where Anne was, he was filled with an overwhelming sense of loneliness.

After the meal he wandered around Soho, past the glaring lights of the strip joints, the fleapits showing blue movies and past the slot machine arcades. Amid the sordid scene of vice of the swinging city Joe felt more alone than ever. He was approached by prostitutes, male and female alike, pestered by touts, and encouraged to enter various brothels. But all failed to interest him. He walked on and on, zombie-like, through the West End, all the way back to the East End, keeping as near to the river as possible. At least the air from the river felt fresh and clean.

At three in the morning, he reached Billingsgate fish market where he stopped at a stall which was doing a roaring trade handing out hot dogs and sandwiches. He bought some coffee and, clutching the thick steaming mug, he sat on a low wall to watch the hustle and bustle of the early morning market trade.

As daylight dawned the cold grey skies formed a background for those ancient buildings of London, giving the grey stone a rosy hue. Silver fish scales glowed on the strange flat leather caps that the fish porters wore. A tall man ran nimbly by with a pyramid of fish boxes balanced precariously on the top of his head. Inside, the fish were alive, a squirming mass. All around, fishy-smelling men pushed little barrows and yelled loudly.

Joe placed the cup on the wall and rummaged in his pocket for his drawing pad and pencil. Leaning against a brick wall, he began to draw the sights before him. Immediately that feeling of melancholy was lifted. Gradually he became happy and calm once more as his hand moved quickly and expertly across the paper. So absorbed was he in his task that he did not notice a lorry that had slowed down in front of him. A curly head poked out of the driver's cab and yelled, 'Why, if it ain't old Joe!'

Joe looked up to the sound of grinding brakes. The next thing he knew his arm was being pumped up and down as his old cell-mate John shook his hand in greeting. 'Hello, Joe,' he said. 'Long time no see, me old mate. I'd know you anywhere, me old cobber from the hill.

'Pop aboard, Joe, I've got a delivery up the road. We'll get some breakfast there,' declared John.

In the van, John looked Joe up and down. 'Same old Joe, arty crafty old bugger.' He laughed. 'When I saw you in the market I thought you was one of those old dead beats that hung out early mornings. It gave me quite a shock when under all that trash there was me old mate Joe.'

In the humorous manner that Joe had loved so well,

young John rambled on, driving towards East India Docks. Soon they were seated in a very clean little café in Limehouse, eating eggs and bacon.

Joe's spirits had lifted. Seeing John felt like coming home. It was as though someone had lighted a fire under him. His mild grey eyes smiled and from the thin hairy face his teeth showed in a jolly grin.

'That's better, me old mate,' said John. 'Yer can't beat some decent grub. How have you been?'

'I'm okay, young John,' replied Joe, 'and even better now that I've met you.'

'So you're not on the floor, mate,' said John with concern. 'Thought you were when I saw the get-up and you hanging about down the market.'

Joe smiled. 'No, I'm all right,' he said. 'I've gone back to work, and I like to draw from real life.'

'I'm me own boss now,' John informed him. 'See me old lorry? She's mine. Borrowed the money for the deposit from me uncle, and I've got to work like a dog to pay for it. Still, I get by, I don't mind what I carry as long as it's honest and well-paid. I don't ever take chances. You can't beat a good honest living. I have to admit I was happy out with the boys, but that's over. And I don't never go down the East End no more unless I deliver to the markets.' He laughed, showing those fine even white teeth.

Joe was delighted. How good it was to meet this lively youth once more. John had always given him great pleasure. But he held something back. He felt he should not tell John the truth about his situation or about Queenie.

'You working, Joe?' John asked.

'Yes, in an office, from nine to five,' Joe lied. 'This sketching is just a hobby.'

'I'm not making a fortune,' John was keen to tell him, 'but at least I'm going straight and that pleases

Marie. Why don't you come and visit us? She's always asking if I've seen you.'

Joe nodded. 'Well, I might just do that, John boy,' he said. 'I'd like that.' He loved this happy lad, it was so great to see him again.

'Come over next weekend, Joe. I could meet you next Friday. I'll pick you up from this café on my way home from work. I come here on a Friday night to deliver and the old Chinamen rustle up some smashing Chinese grub for me.'

Joe was pleased to see John in such good form, taking life in his stride and a strong determination to go straight and provide the good things in life for his family. He felt a little ashamed of the way he had lied to John about working in an office. John had accepted this lie without question.

'If you come next weekend,' John continued, 'we can take the kids fishing – that's how I spend my Sundays. It's nice out Epping way, plenty of woods and scenery. You'd like it.'

Joe hesitated, thinking of the complications of getting too friendly with John again. He must not involve the young boy with the firm, that was certain, since the boys would probably have a disruptive effect on him. Easy money was always a great temptation.

But Joe's loneliness made him selfish. He loved young John so why should he not continue the friendship? Slowly he began to work out how he might have his way without jeopardising John's plans. John and Marie did not need to be told of Queenie, and John was not likely to return to his old haunts – the strong-minded little woman he married would see to that.

'That's kind of you,' Joe heard himself saying.

'Right, me old mate,' returned John, 'Marie will be chuffed. I hope you're going to stay the whole week-end. Got to go now, I'll pick you up next Friday.'

With a last jolly wave and infectious grin, John and his battered old fishy-smelling lorry were soon out of sight.

Joe waved goodbye feeling much more light-hearted and made his way home to his dreary attic. Once installed there he began to think of Queenie downstairs. He felt tempted in some ways but he was determined to have no more to do with that moody nymphomaniac. He locked his door and had a good night's rest.

The first member of the gang came home in the morning when Joe was cleaning up in the bar. It was Pickles. He spotted Joe and signalled for him to join him for a drink. The husky lad's usually ruddy face was pallid. He was wearing a smart lightweight suit but it was stained and rumpled as if he had been in it all night. Over his shoulder he carried a pair of binoculars. 'Well, Yos, how's tricks?' His greeting was casual.

'Just the same,' replied Joe looking with interest at this hefty lad in his crumpled finery, and thinking that greasy overalls suited him better.

'Took me for a ride, those bleeding bookies did,' muttered Pickles once he had downed his pint of ale.

'Don't tell me you gambled all your money away,' said Joe in astonishment.

'Skinned me alive, they did,' complained Pickles. 'I'll be bloody glad to get in me garage and get this gear off. Ain't been bleeding warm since I took me overalls off.' He shivered in a very depressed manner.

Joe was amazed at the way this well-built youth had eagerly defied the law and risked a long prison sentence and yet was fish out of the water away from the gang. Money did him no good at all.

Towards evening Snatcher returned in an even

worse condition. 'I'm going to have a kip on your bed, Yos,' he muttered as he wandered vacantly past him. There were huge bags under his eyes and his shoulders were hunched like those of an old man.

'Trouble?' asked Joe.

'No, just a bird, and a bloody expensive one, too,' he grumbled.

So the boys came home to roost like bedraggled pigeons. They all gathered in the office every day, littering Joe's home with cigarette ends and empty beer bottles. They played cards together and occasionally gawped with loud noises of appreciation at huge pornographic blow-ups brought back from their haunts in the West End.

Joe was rather relieved when Friday finally came around. He wore his best shirt and freshly pressed trousers. He paid a visit to the barber to have all his whiskers removed and to get a stylish haircut. For some reason he had a feeling that John's wife Marie would appreciate these efforts.

Everything was just as he had imagined in John and Marie's home. It was as neat and pretty as a doll's house. Marie had greeted him warmly and affectionately. She was wearing a blue nylon overall which matched her cornflower eyes. She had one bonny baby girl in a pram and the little boy, who had John's merry brown eyes, ran happily all over the house.

It was the most pleasant weekend Joe had spent for many years. He was very happy, though constantly reminded of Anne, with the supper table so carefully laid, the neatly arranged bowl of flowers, the candles in the centre of the table. These were all things Anne used to like to have. Being with John and Marie was a glimpse of the past, an elusive memory that had gone from his life.

John took him to the bus stop on Sunday night. 'Do come again soon, Joe,' he said. 'Marie likes you. You are her type – an intellectual, not an ignoramus like me.' He laughed but there was a hint of regret in his voice.

Joe put a hand on his shoulder. 'Johnny boy, you suit each other well,' he said. 'You are a very fine couple, don't you ever think otherwise.

As Joe headed back to Queenie's Castle, his heart felt heavy. The happiness John had found made him feel quite envious. Joe's marriage in New York had been such a miserable one, he had lost all confidence in domesticity. And even when he knew his feelings for Anne were genuine ones, he had insisted that they live in separate rooms, so anxious was he to protect himself from disappointment again. But seeing John and Marie had given him renewed hope. There would have been something good with Anne, but now she was gone. Perhaps he would find another woman one day or perhaps he might even be able to track down Anne again, if she hadn't already been claimed by another man. There was no good reason to hope that she was waiting for Joe.

With these confused thoughts in his head, Joe went back to the place of vice that was his home.

Chapter Fourteen

Another Raid

On Monday the Hustler arrived back from Spain looking very suntanned. Doug also returned from his visit to the Emerald Isle, his tubby belly extended further by the amount of Guinness he had consumed. He rubbed his stomach. 'Me old dutch likes to go home once in a while,' he said, 'but Christ that Irish beer don't arf upset me.'

By evening Spinx's loud voice could be heard in the bar and the gang was complete. It was time to plan another job.

Once again the gang members draped themselves around the office. Puffing a large cigar the boss sat in his high-back red chair and desk. Every now and then he would pour himself a tumbler of whisky and gulp it down.

Joe leaned on the wide windowsill which reflected the ripples of the river below, and thought how much bluer the boss's nose looked. His voice was also exceedingly hoarse as though he had imbibed a lot of alcohol recently. As loud and bombastic as ever, Spinx waved his large hands as he explained the instructions for the next job to be carried out by the firm.

'This time, lads,' he said, 'we are going to take a big chance. We'll do two jobs in a row – one each night and then the pay-off.'

The boys all looked with interest but no one commented.

'It will be a bit dodgy,' Spinx continued, 'but not if it's well planned and you bastards don't start getting lazy. If it's carefully planned, there's no reason why we shouldn't get away with it.'

Having delivered his long speech, he then relaxed back in his chair and handed Joe a large foolscap sheet of paper. 'Study that, Yossel,' he ordered. 'It's only a rough sketch. I want you to get it into shape. It's two city offices near London Wall. They collect their payroll Thursday and pay out on Friday. We'll do two jobs, one on Thursday night and the other on early morning Friday. From Monday on we start casing the joint. That gives Joe a few days to make a good map of the district.'

'Yes, boss,' the boys all answered in unison.

'Right, well that's it. We meet again Saturday night to get the last details. That'll give Joe a few days to sort out the plan. And now, you bastards,' he roared, 'who wants a sub?' His great hand withdrew his wallet from his jacket pocket and handed them twenty pounds each. 'Put it in the book, Joe,' he said. 'Don't want no welshing,' he jested.

So they all disappeared, leaving only smoke and whisky fumes behind them. As Joe carefully looked at the plan, he thought about how easily they came by their money and how incredibly quickly they spent it. He had scrimped and scraped all his life to buy books to educate himself in order to pass on his learning to gormless kids who mostly only concerned themselves with sex or pop music. What a fool he had been! What a waste of time! It was time he learned the error of his ways. Easy come easy go was the pattern of life down here beside the Thames. From now on it was going to be his way too. After all, what was a conscience?

Only a guilty complex that could quite easily be cured . . .

At the next meeting he met Enricho, or Flash, another member of the gang. He was a slim, dark boy who carried a camera over his shoulder. He arrived with large blow-up shots taken from all angles of a merchant bank in the city. These were all passed around for everyone to look at carefully. Joe learned that Enricho's profession was that of a roaming freelance photographer, the kind that pestered tourists exploring London. He was very useful to the gang.

For the rest of the week, Joe worked very conscientiously on the map. Using Flash's photographs of the building and its surroundings, he spent almost a whole day in the shadow of that ancient Roman wall sketching the blocks of offices to make sure that fire escapes and windows were all in the right positions.

This time he felt quite fired up about the job. He was definitely interested. This feeling of the excitement of a new adventure had not been with him since his youth.

Doug's stocky shape pottered about in front of the bank. He had got himself a job decorating the building. Occasionally Snatcher passed by in his taxi-cab giving him the thumbs-up sign. Having discarded his roll-necked jersey, the Hustler cased the joint in a dark suit as a bank manager, while Spinx, with Pickles as his chauffeur, masqueraded as a rich customer.

Joe was quietly impressed by the immense planning that went on, the working out of every minute detail. It was hard not to admire their skill. A little voice tried to remind Joe that they were rogues and villains and they were defying the law, but his admiration remained. He was hooked himself. He had begun to think with the mind of a criminal and could see little that was wrong with it.

When Joe's large map was completed it was pinned to the wall. Then every street corner, lamp-post and telephone kiosk was carefully added. It was incredible how carefully and diligently the job was planned. The class was attentive and alert again as each one received their final instructions. Looking at the photographs, Joe noticed that Pickles sat wearing his chauffeur's cap at the wheel of a big Daimler parked almost outside the bank and that Doug was up a ladder cleaning windows.

'Get the idea, Joe?' Spinx asked. 'We've been casing this joint for weeks, but I don't want no muck-ups with the roads, like last time. That's what we want the maps for. Old Bill keeps changing the signs and it's not as easy to get away as it used to be. It's a one-way street one day and no entry the next. I want it all kept up to date, with no slip-ups. I know what I'm doing, I know me job, but the rest of the lads have got to have it drummed into their bleeding thick heads.'

Thus each man was given his specific part by Spinx as though a great drama production were being put on. 'Snatcher drives a minicab in the day so he keeps us in touch with the traffic problems, and then he takes the car on the night. Me, Doug and Hustler do the job. Pickles will be there with a van, like that, the money goes in one direction and not in another. Hustler's Pop's a look-out and you, Joe, you hang onto the end of the phone in case of trouble.'

He pointed to the telephone on top of the desk. It had two lines – an outside line and an extension to the bar.

'Now, it's all settled,' he said. 'Next Thursday,

then. If we go over the top get back to your jobs, lads, and keep your noses clean.'

'Stick by the phone for the next few days, Joe,' Spinx said to him, 'just in case the boys need help. Queenie's the only one who knows where to find me.' Spinx had finished. Now he relaxed and started on the usual bottle.

'They're a good bunch of lads,' Spinx told Joe when the others had all left. 'We don't make a fortune but we keep out of trouble. I don't believe in violence, we don't use no shooters and coshes. We got a couple of hefty lads if there is trouble and I can still take care of myself.' He clutched a big fist. 'You'll get your cut again, Joe,' he said, 'but of course it won't be as much as the lads that's outside. But as I say, it's often the smaller details that get overlooked and that's your job. Keep an eye on that desk, stay by the phone and don't let no sod come up here no matter who he says he is.'

The whisky loosened Spinx's tongue and during that conversation Joe learned that the Hustler's sensitive hands could usually open any safe, but failing that Spinx was the best blower in the business. He learned that Snatcher could lose the entire police force in a car chase, and that Doug and Pickles were tough musclemen.

'Should you happen to get a message from the Queen,' continued Spinx, 'one that says that the heat's on, that means that Old Bill is prowling about down in the bar. Keep out of sight then. Queenie can handle them but should you at any time get a message to say that the lid's off, then scarper. Hide yourself under the bloody arches, anywhere, till you get a signal that it's all clear.' His hard little eyes subjected Joe to a piercing scrutiny. 'Well,' he went on, 'we all got to trust each other. Here's the key to the desk.' He placed a key up on the old beams.

'Only we know where that's hid, so keep it to yourself, Yos. Now, don't forget – if, and only if, you get the word that the lid's come off, you take the bag out of the desk and stay hidden until Hustler's Pop finds you. There are plenty of places about here. And don't try nothing, Yos,' he warned, 'or the boys won't like it. In that bag is the kitty from the last job. I don't pay the lads out in hot money – we can't take chances like that.'

After Spinx had gone, Joe lay on his bed. He felt quite exhilarated, it all seemed so thrilling and exciting. That night he went to sleep with strange stirrings of excitement in his belly. He felt like a kid looking forward to a party.

The next day Joe had lunch with sweet Nelly who was very hot and flustered as she chatted non-stop about her recent visit to see her husband in the nick. These trips to the island were the only breaks she ever had in her hard-working life, the excitement of each one lasting until visiting time came round again.

'I looked very smart,' she said. 'He was pleased. I wore a nice brick-coloured two piece, I did, and had me hair done, too.'

'I'm sure you looked lovely, Nelly,' Joe grinned affectionately at her as she banged down the bowl of flour. Up to her elbows, she mixed the pudding for the next day and still rambled on.

'Met some of the girls, I did. Theresa still goes, and so does Tilly, but Sandra's got a bloke, and she's turned it in.'

Joe looked at her in mild surprise but merrily she chattered on.

'Gawd, I don't know if I could stand it, thirty bloody years. Blimey, five's been too many for me.'

Joe realised that she was talking about one of the wives of the long-term prisoners. A little shudder went through him. Next time he could be one of them . . . Well, at least it would be for something he was guilty of this time. Last time it had been for someone else's crime, he thought bitterly.

'You are quiet today, Joe,' Nelly said, stopping her chatter and looking at him in concern.

'I'm okay, Nelly,' Joe said, revealing his teeth in that jolly grin that was reserved for his sweet friend.

Nelly lowered her voice. 'Don't want to let the missus worry you,' she whispered. 'It would be a waste of time.'

Joe smiled gently. Astute little Nelly. She knew everything that went on at Queenie's Castle.

'Tell me, Nelly,' he said, 'why is Queenie so temperamental and changeable?'

'She's scared,' whispered Nelly.

'Of whom?' he asked.

'The old Gaffer, of course,' replied Nelly.

'But he's in prison,' said Joe rather surprised. He paused and then added, 'And I'm not the only one who gets into her bed.'

'Come outside into the scullery,' said Nelly wiping her hand on a towel. 'Give me a hand with the dishes and I'll put you in the picture.' Her voice had dropped as if she were afraid of being overheard.

In the narrow confines of the scullery, the little back room where the pots were washed, they stood close together amid the steam from the greasy washing-up water.

'You know that I've known Queenie a long time,' said Nelly, 'ever since she was a kid playing down our street. Her mother run off with a Yank and her father got topped by the race gangs. At twelve she was running wild and at fifteen she was on the game. The old Gaffer owned her then, and she worked in his rotten dirty club.' Nelly's voice was shaky. She sounded angry. Joe looked quizzically at her.

'You know,' Nelly raised her eyebrows. 'It was one of those soup kitchens, or brothels, whatever they call them.'

As always, Nelly's humour amused Joe. He chuckled. 'But she never goes to visit the Gaffer in prison, does she?' he asked.

'No,' replied Nelly, 'but he bought this pub for her and there is plenty down here what does visit him. He's Jack the Lad down there. Queenie's life won't be worth tuppence if he gets out and finds she's done the dirty on him. It was the same for any woman the Gaffer went with before he got nicked. Queenie was very jealous and made trouble for anyone who went near her man. But now she's been cheating on the Gaffer and there'll be big trouble, I can tell you. So you see, Joe, it's safety in numbers for her. She can't afford to like anyone, yet she needs a bloody man more than anyone I know.' Nelly stacked the pots on the draining board.

After that enlightening conversation with Nelly, Joe felt slightly better but still a trifle bewildered. Now he knew there was definitely a strong bond between Queenie and the Gaffer. And it was certain too that Queenie's interest in Joe himself only existed for sex. Her special talents in bed that had made him feel so special were simply a result of a lifetime of prostitution. It had nothing to do with any feelings she might have had for him. That would make it easier to distance himself from his feelings and betray her . . .

The day of the next raid was drawing close but Joe found himself in the grip of quite a severe depression. His earlier courage seemed to have deserted him entirely. The success of this job would benefit him financially yet he did not really care about money, having almost forgotten how to spend freely. If the

job failed he might end up with another long prison
sentence. And that would break him.

And so, while Joe had been quite blasé about
success or failure only a few days before, now the
very thought of being shut up for any number of
years made his heart beat fast with terrible fear. Most
decidedly he was trapped. There was no way out.

On Saturday, everyone was briefed upstairs for the
final rehearsal for Thursday's raid and then the gang
settled down for a nice steady drink in the bar
downstairs. But as they say, there is no rest for the
wicked. Just before ten o'clock, the front door of the
bar burst open and a group of men rushed in, led by a
fat oaf who wielded a sledgehammer. With war cries,
he charged into battle, swinging the sledgehammer
about his head. With every swipe, a chair or a table
was smashed to the floor. Women screamed and the
other customers cowered against the wall.

'It's Fatso, it's Fatso,' someone yelled. Some
screaming girls rushed into the toilets, while several
of the men clashed in battle like buffalo bulls.

Joe had fled into a hiding place behind the door. The
last thing he was going to do was fight. Nervously he
gripped the woodwork to hold the door shut. Queenie
was pacing up and down the bar with a string of oaths
pouring from her mouth. A pot plant sailed through
the air, glasses crashed to the floor. All the noise
added to the excitement of the brawl, but Joe was
horrified. Violence had always filled him with terror.
Even seeing the fights in prison had not cured him
of that. So he was now both a moral and a physical
coward.

Sweating hard, Joe continued to hide behind the
door as he waited for the fights to subside. Then
he heard the shrill sound of sirens in the distance.
The police cars were on their way. Now he could
hear Queenie's voice above the shouts as she clanged

the ship's bell vigorously. 'Stop it, you bastards!' she
called. 'Someone has sent for the Old Bill.'

The tone of her voice suggested to Joe that the
greatest crime that someone committed that evening
was informing the police.

Almost immediately, the assailants parted and the
intruders dashed for the door. Doug was rescued
from the floor and Spinx put his jacket back on.
Queenie calmly smoothed her blonde hair as the
police entered, and with a charming half-smile went
forward to greet them.

Joe watched the way she dealt with them in fasci-
nation. There were three constables, one of whom
had a notebook. They wanted names, descriptions,
addresses, anything they could get. Queenie made
sure that they got nothing.

'Oh dear, I'm so glad you came. I was so scared
but they cleared off when they heard the cars coming.'
With a sweet smile Queenie explained how these
young lads had broken in and proceeded to wreck
the place. No, she did not know them, she told the
police. They were all strangers to the district.

The neatly dressed young constable wrote earnestly
in his notebook, taking in every detail.

Bending to the floor, Queenie exclaimed, 'Oh, look
at my plants.' She picked up the shattered pot plant
tenderly. 'What's wrong with these lads?' she asked
innocently. 'It was just as well my uncle was staying, I
don't know what would have happened otherwise.'

'Never mind, madam,' the young constable assured
her. 'We will see that they don't come back.' He was
obviously taken in by her manner.

The constables were very considerate and clearly
enjoyed being entertained by such a charming hostess.
'A glass of beer, officers?' she tempted them.

'Well, unfortunately, madam, we're on duty,' the
constable replied.

'Well, I won't tell anyone,' Queenie said, fluttering her long eyelashes at them.

Listening to the conversation, Joe was impressed by the way Queenie handled those men. Then, while the police were tucking in to their beer, Queenie edged over to where Joe was huddled. 'Beat it upstairs,' she hissed. 'And lock the door, Joe, just in case they decide to poke about.'

Joe slipped away and spent the rest of the evening in his locked quarters. It was astonishing to him that Queenie should want to protect the gang that had attacked her bar, even though she knew who they were. What a strange moral code they had . . .

It turned out that the gang who had attacked the Queen's Castle was a rival gang from the other side of town and well known to all. It seemed that they too were planning a job in that area and wanted no competition. But not one word of their identity was given to the police. It was against their principles. Queenie was certainly the real Queen of this castle of crime.

Soon Queenie's Castle had forgotten about the gang fight. At the time it had caused a lot of gossip and there had been long discussions by the locals about the two gangs. A few bandaged heads remained but for the boys in the 'office' there were far more important things to discuss as they prepared for the raid.

Chapter Fifteen

The Pay-off

There was little sunset to break the gloom that evening while Joe sat waiting by the phone, as he had been instructed to do. It had been raining all day and the sky was grey and overcast. Joe whiled away the last hour of daylight with a swift sketch of Hustler's Pop hanging furtively at the street corner rolling that thin everlasting fag which was then allowed to droop, unlit, from his lips. Hustler's Pop turned his head to and fro like some old grey rat watching his prey.

Once it was dark and he could no longer see from the window, Joe lay on the bed in that dim room, wondering how he would ever get himself out of this mesh of crime he had become involved in. If only he had some hint about who had killed Maisie. But this was such a closed shop. No one ever talked of the past. Their minds always dwelt on the present.

While staying at Queenie's, Joe had often walked miles in a vain attempt to find that dingy café or even that fatal back alley where young Maisie had been done to death. But since that time, developers had made a clean sweep of the district. There was not one familiar sign. There were only large cranes and wooden hoardings as massive blocks of sky-high flats were erected. At Queenie's, Joe knew that he was in the right place. All criminal connections seemed to lead to this place, this den of iniquity named the Ship and Castle, alias Queenie's Bar. In his wilder moments, Joe thought about turning copper's nark in an attempt to clear his own name, but he knew that was a stupid idea and much too dangerous. Queenie's friends would make short work of a grass.

The hours ticked by. *The job should have been done by now*, he thought. *Where were they?* He hoped nothing had gone wrong. Now he was getting nervous. He began to sweat. Suddenly in the distance he heard the high piercing sound of police car sirens. Joe's heart gave a terrific leap. Suddenly the phone rang and he almost fell off the bed. Jumping up, he grabbed the receiver and a gruff voice said, 'Lid's off, Yossel, you know the drill.'

For a moment Joe hesitated as he tried to remember what he had to do. Then, panic-stricken, he rushed over to grab the key and unlock the desk. Bundling all the papers into an old briefcase, he took out the battered suitcase which contained the pay-off. Turning off the light, he made for the back door. But when he got there he found something was blocking the doorway. It was moving and groaning. Then it tried to crawl over the step but sank back exhausted. Joe put down the suitcase and rushed over to pick up the blood-stained body of Snatcher who was wallowing in his own blood. Through his swollen, injured lips, he muttered, 'Blow, Yossel, Old Bill's down below.'

But Joe dragged him inside. He shot the bolts on the door, and pulled him onto the bed. Tearing up the sheets, he staunched the wounds on his body. There had obviously been a car accident. Huge pieces of glass were embedded in his face and hands. Joe carefully removed a sliver of glass that was in danger of penetrating Snatcher's eye. The boy had now passed out. Joe was so intent on trying to stop the flow of blood that he did not notice that Spinx and Doug had crept up the fire escape and were now standing beside him.

'Crickey! The boy's in a bad way,' whispered Spinx. He wrapped Snatcher up in the bedcover and picked him up in those strong arms as if the lad were a baby. 'Go warn yer missus we're coming,' he said to Doug. Doug ran off swiftly and quietly in his plimsolled feet.

'Pick up the case, Joe,' Spinx said softly. 'Don't make a sound. Queenie will let us out the side door. Old Bill's prowling about the back.'

They hurried swiftly down the stairs and out of the side door into the little street. Within minutes they were in the small house where Doug lived. In the front room downstairs with its immaculate curtained windows and clean white bed, Spinx installed the unconscious Snatcher on the sofa.

Doug's wife, Bernadette, was a pretty woman with blue-black hair and a soft Irish brogue. 'Oh, bejasus, poor lad,' she exclaimed. She had busied herself getting hot water and bandages ready. Now she examined him. There were no bones broken, she said, just deep cuts. 'You boys get going,' she said. 'I'll get old Doc Sullivan to put a stitch or two in him.'

With her soft voice and professional manner, she took over without any fuss.

Spinx opened the front door. 'Come along, lads,' he ordered. 'Pickles is back. Let's get away.'

In a very old van driven by the red-haired giant, they careered through the night. For all its years, the van was capable of terrific speed, the engine having been doctored and expertly tuned. Rather morosely the boys discussed the raid, and told Joe what had happened.

'Pulled it off all right, we did,' said the boss, 'but

some stupid sod in another office block spotted us and gave the alarm. Spud got up river with the loot and Doug and I went with Pickles in the van, while Snatcher, Hustler and Flash led the coppers off the trail in a nicked car driven by Snatcher. But his luck ran out. Some drunk stepped off the kerb in front of him, he swerved, hit a parked car and turned over. As far as I know, the other boys have made a run for it. They got to Snatcher before the cops got there, and left him down by the fire escape I just hope they made it. Good lads, they are. I wouldn't like to lose them,' he said.

Their destination was a spot by a river. Joe did not like to ask where but it was here that they made a rendezvous with the elusive Spud. He stepped out of the shadows and signalled to them with a lighted torch.

The night had become cold, wet and windy and the dawn was not far away. Joe heard the distinct chug chug of a boat on the river.

'Off you all go,' said Spinx, as he got on the boat. 'Don't come back till you get the all-clear. Hang about Jane's.'

Jane's turned out to be a riverside hotel of the sort that serves early breakfast to enthusiastic all-night fishermen. Jane gave the men hot coffee and eggs and bacon. She was a robust middle-aged woman with the typical hard face of an East-Ender. She showed no surprise and very little interest at the arrival of the early morning guests. In a taciturn manner she offered them the services of the bathroom, and then went about her own business with solid indifference. At midday they were still installed at Jane's. Pickles and Doug played on the fruit machines and Joe sat huddled in a corner to keep out of the draught. The wind seemed to blow with a gale force about the ramshackle building. Outside the river looked cold and grey. In fact the whole atmosphere was damp. He yawned and wished for his warm bed. Suddenly the sleepy rural silence was disturbed by the phone and the high-pitched tones of Hustler's Pop came over the wire. 'Okay, boys, you can come home now,' he said.

Soon they were travelling back to London and Joe crept wearily into bed. The night was not over for Pickles. His instructions were to help remove Snatcher from Doug's house and take him to a posh bird's flat in Chelsea where, for a price, she had agreed to hide him.

And while the Queen got ready to deal with the coppers, Joe lay upstairs in bed, mentally and physically exhausted.

Chapter Sixteen

The Lion of the Law

The great British lion of the law often lies sleeping soundly until one small thing disturbs him. Distinct rumblings are likely to be heard as he wakes up, and then with a loud roar, he bounds into action.

Certainly now the police had realised that there was something decidedly fishy going on down by the river, and it did not just concern fish. There was a certain area down there which badly needed investigation.

Two flying squad officers had handed in an interesting report of some goings-on the night before. They had received an emergency call to a shipping office in the city but arrived too late to make any arrests. There they had discovered the safe blown and the elaborate burglar alarm system neatly dismantled. The ten thousand pounds pay roll had gone missing. It was a neat, professional job. Another squad car had chased a stolen vehicle in the vicinity of the crime through a maze of narrow city streets but then lost it near Tower Bridge. At almost the same time, the traffic police had been called out to an accident concerning a car that had careered down a narrow street buffeting other parked cars and turning on its side. The driver and its passengers had run off and disappeared down the back streets. One was clearly injured because they left a trail of blood, but so far no trace of him had been found.

Superintendent Mackenzie was studying all these reports in the local police station and scratching his semi–bald pate where his red hair had receded over the years. 'Something's going on down there,' he muttered.

His assistant, Terry Long, looked up. He was a smart, supercilious young man who looked at his superior with silent contempt. The old man had started talking to himself now, he thought.

'I'm pretty sure I know who did this job,' muttered Mackenzie, 'but I thought I'd rooted out that lot when I nicked the Gaffer.'

He got to his feet, went over to the wall and stared up at a large map of the district. His tired red-veined eyes peered closely at it, and then taking a pencil, he ringed a small section of it. 'That's it,' he said, turning to stare sombrely at the ambitious lad who was waiting so impatiently to step into his shoes when he retired.

'Come over here, son,' he ordered. 'Take a peek at this.' He sucked his lower lip as his assistant stood beside him. 'You don't know that area,' Mackenzie said, 'but I do. I used to be a young bobby on the beat down there.'

Terry Long tried very hard not to look bored but there were times when the super's constant references to the old days really got on his nerves.

'Five safe blow-outs in a row,' muttered the superintendent. 'And that is where the trouble is.' He pointed to the map. 'Queenie's Castle. I'll bet my last bob on it.'

The young detective shifted his feet unsteadily. 'Queenie's Castle,' he repeated. 'What is that?'

'It's a boozer,' declared Mackenzie belligerently, 'and it's run by a woman, but *what* a woman!' He grinned as though recalling some past joke. 'Ah,' he said sitting down and lighting up his pipe, 'those were the days, when coppers' private lives were their own affair. I remember my super, old Fisher. Queenie used to be his bit of crumpet, she did.' Mackenzie puffed away savouring those old memories.

Terry Long remained silent. He may have despised Red Mac but he never argued with him. He valued his job too much, and was looking forward to promotion.

'I want all recent police reports concerning that district brought here. Anything – whether it's petty larceny, brawls, indecent exposure. I want the whole bloody lot. We're going to be very busy for the next few days.' An amused grin appeared on Mackenzie's face again as if he were recalling some interesting memories of the past.

The investigation continued for several days. Red Mac briefed his young staff of the past daring deeds committed in the dark alleys that had now disappeared, the romping grounds of his youth, that area of the riverside between Stepney and Wapping. 'It's bred in these lads,' he told them, 'from father to son, they live by having a little fiddle from the docks and a bit of black market in wartime. But the particular hoodlum I have in mind at the moment has an excellent war record – special commando service. He was taught how to crack a safe as easily as opening a tin can.'

'So you think he's still active,' remarked Terry Long, a little sarcastically.

Mackenzie turned to him. 'There's no need to be so cocky, my lad,' he said. 'There's plenty of us still around, as you so tactfully put it.'

'Now,' continued Mackenzie, 'according to the report of last night's raid, the bank employed a new maintenance man two weeks beforehand. Listen to this description: fiftyish with battered features and cauliflower ears. If that ain't old Billy Douglas, I'll eat my old trilby hat.' Red Mac leaned back very satisfied. 'Yes, that Jim Spinx and Billy Douglas are back in action. I think we'll pay the Queen a surprise visit.'

It was very evident to all concerned that not only was the old super going to visit this famous queen of the underworld, but he was also going to see her alone.

Leaving Terry Long and two young constables sitting in the squad car thirty yards down the road, Mackenzie strolled leisurely down to Queenie's Bar.

It was the lunch hour and the general hubbub of eating and drinking was under way. Queenie was looking more glamorous than ever in an emerald green jersey suit. Rhinestones gleamed at her neckline and with her blonde hair set to perfection, she perched on her stool sending out charming little smiles in all directions. There was a momentary tightening of her hand around the glass as Red Mac walked in but that was all the emotion she displayed.

With his neat stocky figure, hard felt hat, and florid features, there was little to distinguish Mackenzie from the row of shipping clerks and bank managers who lined the bar. But she knew him all right.

'Hello, Mac,' she said in a soft voice. 'Long time no see.'

Mac patted her arm. 'Hello, pet, what are you having?'

'The usual, Mac, gin and tonic.'

A quiet drama was being acted out between them but those city workers would never have guessed it from the cool cat-like gaze of the Queen, or the jolly, pleasant attitude of Red Mac.

'I must say, Queenie, you're wearing very well,' he said.

'Give over, Mac,' she replied with a cosy smile. 'I'm still on the good side of thirty. Anyway, what are you doing here? Nothing ever happens now. It's dull as ditch water since you nabbed the Gaffer.'

Mackenzie did not reply instantly. He just stared hard at her and then allowed his gaze to travel around the bar. Looking up with interest at the portrait over the bar, he said, 'A good likeness, that. Who did it? Some ex-con, no doubt.'

'Could be,' Queenie murmured with that same enigmatic smile on her lips. 'Come on, Mac,' she urged him. 'Tell me what you're looking for. I might be able to help.'

Mackenzie was wary: he knew Queenie would never be a grass.

'I just popped in for a drink,' he explained. 'I like to see the old haunts. I'm retiring after Christmas.'

'How nice,' returned Queenie with a faint hint of irony. 'You don't want to buy a pub, do you? I'm right cheesed off with this one.'

'No, love,' Mackenzie said kindly. 'My garden and my dog will be enough excitement for me.' As he spoke, his keen eyes noticed Hustler's Pop put his head round the door and scuttle out again. 'So long, love,' he said. 'Take care.' He bade a fond farewell to the Queen and hurried out to see what that little rat was up to.

But he had already missed the main drama outside, when the wounded Snatcher had been secreted out of Doug's house and into Pickles's van, so heavily bandaged that he was unrecognisable. The van door had already been slammed shut and the old vehicle had charged down the street. Hustler's Pop had returned to his usual pitch, just as Mackenzie approached. He greeted the policeman with his usual cocky grin. 'Hello, Squire, out of bounds, ain't yer?'

'Hello, Sam,' said Mackenzie affably. 'Still pitching? I thought street bookies were finished.'

'Just can't lose the habit, I reckon,' replied Hustler's Pop, who had been known in the old days as Slippery Sam. 'It's all bleeding betting shops since you blokes made it legal,' he complained.

Mackenzie stuffed his hands into his overcoat pockets and stood looking about him casually. 'How are Jim Spinx and Billy Douglas these days? Still living in the manor?' He fired this question at the shrewd little crook before him, looking down at his long thin nose and those small mean eyes which looked meaner than ever. They also looked shifty.

'Never see Jim Spinx,' muttered Hustler's Pop. 'He moved out of London. As for Billy Douglas, he's been going straight for years, he has. Got a window-cleaning round.'

'You don't say,' replied Mackenzie, looking quite unconcerned as his keen eyes scanned the street. Not like old times down here, is it?'

'You're right there, guv'nor. It's pretty dull down here now,' replied Hustler's Pop.

Mackenzie put his fingers to his lips and whistled down the squad car which had been cruising round the block. For a moment there was a fleeting look of fear on Hustler's Pop's face as the car drew up. But as Mackenzie opened the door and climbed in, he drew a sigh of relief.

'Crickey!' he muttered as he watched the police drive off. 'Now what has brought that slimy git out of his hole?'

Inside the squad car, Mackenzie smirked. 'She's the same old Queenie,' he said. 'Sweet as a sugar plum.'

Terry Long sniffed. 'I sometimes wonder whose side you're on,' he said in his supercilious tone of voice.

Mackenzie's bloodshot eyes blazed with temper.

'I know what bloody side I'm on,' he shouted. 'I would never have survived twenty years and kept me bloody nose clean otherwise. Let's hope you can do the same.'

Chapter Seventeen

The Grass

On Monday Spinx called an important meeting of the firm in which he informed them all that it would be better to cool it for a while.

'That old Mackenzie is like a bloodhound,' he said. 'Once he gets the scent, he never gives up. We'll do our last job on Thursday. Seeing as we've spent so much time and money casing the joint, we might as well. And I've just received some good inside information.' He grinned. 'There's going to be sparklers in that safe on Thursday night. Some old dame whose husband is on the board of the bank is coming over from France for a special do. She always puts her sparklers in the office safe at night. So how's that?' A murmur of assent went around the room. Though Joe stood silent at the back, with a little frown of worry creasing his brow.

'Now, lads,' continued Spinx. 'If we get our hands on those sparklers we'll be able to afford to lay off for quite a while – at least until old Mackenzie retires or snuffs it.'

'We'll be a man short,' said Doug.

'Well, Pickles can take Snatcher's place,' said Spinx. 'There's no need to nick a car this time. We'll use the van and then dump it. There'll be a bit of roof-climbing to dismantle the alarm, but Hustler, you can manage that. Now, me and Doug will bust the safe, and we should manage with Flash as a look-out.'

'Why don't we take Yossel?' someone suggested.

Joe felt a nervous twinge at the sound of his pseudonym. The last thing he needed was to be sent out on a job, so he was relieved when Spinx dismissed the idea.

'No,' Spink said. 'We've got to have good inside men, we can't leave it all to the Queen. Anyway, there's still plenty of lolly in the kitty. With a bit of luck, on top of the sparklers, not one of us will have to worry for a year or two.'

After the rest of the gang had dispersed and left, Spinx seemed in an unusually talkative mood as he settled down to his whisky. 'Have a drink, Joe,' he offered.

'No, thanks, boss,' Joe refused. 'I only drink beer. That stuff's too potent for me.'

'Don't know what yer missing,' jested Spinx, refilling his glass. 'I'm nearly sixty, Joe, though I know I don't look it. But it's time I started taking things a bit easy. Besides, me old lady gets a bit upset what with me being away from home so often. I've got a grand little place down in Essex, and it's time we started to enjoy it.'

Joe nodded. It was true that Spinx did not look anywhere close to sixty. 'It's nice that you've found marriage agreeable,' he commented.

'Thirty-five years, boy,' said Spinx with pride. 'We was only kids when we started out, and not a bloody bean between us. We got a son out in Canada and he's got three children. It might be nice to take the old lady on a visit out there.'

'I'm very curious to know if this has always been your way of making a living.' Joe spoke cautiously, slightly afraid of causing offence.

Spinx threw back his head and roared with laughter.
'Seeing as you asked me so nicely, Yossel, I'll tell you,'
he said. 'Yeah, well, it's been on and off. After my
five-year dose of porridge, I went straight for a long
time. Then I went into the army and got real training.
I was a commando in the special service. By the time
I got me demob I could bust open anything and cut a
bloke's throat without turning a hair. But believe me,
Yossel,' he added hastily, 'I've got a clear conscience
there, murders are not my line. I'm crooked, yes, I
like easy money, but I do a clean job. It's like you
with them pictures you draw. I enjoy it. I never done
no gas meters or robbed old folk. I ain't got no time
for petty thieves, I'll never have one in my outfit,' he
boasted.

Behind his thick specs, Joe's eyes gleamed with a
strange emotion. He felt an odd sort of affection for
this big loud man.

'So now I'm pulling out of this racket,' Spinx
continued, 'so it's up to you, Yossel, me lad, to
look out for yourself. I warn you, when the Gaffer
gets out next year, things will be different, and that's
as good a reason as any to blow. Knives and coshes,
it ain't me racket, and as for using bleeding kids to
peddle drugs – pah!' he added in disgust.

Immediately Joe was interested. This was the first
reference to the teenagers who had led him into
trouble on that foggy night. But Spinx had said
his piece, and had got up ready to leave. Fixing Joe with those steady eyes, he said, 'Tell the
Queen to get you fixed up with some dud insurance
cards. If Mackenzie finds you've got form, he'll pick
you up straight away. Call yerself Joe Abrahams,
and say you work behind the bar.' Spinx winked
at him. 'So long, Joe,' he said. 'Remember now,
stick by the phone on Thursday, it's the same
routine, you know the drill. Be seeing you, then.'

And off he went. It was the last time Joe ever saw him.

Down at the police station, Mackenzie stared at the map on the wall with a puzzled expression. 'It's gone very quiet down there. I think something's brewing,' he muttered.

'Why don't you raid the damned place if you think something's going on there?' Terry Long asked somewhat acidly.

Mackenzie grunted. 'Don't be a fool, man, these are professionals. The joint will be as clean as a whistle by the time you flatfoots get there.'

Terry Long gave a nonchalant shrug. He was getting more fed up and impatient with the super every day. He stared with annoyance at the superintendent's bald pate, now half obscured by the clouds of smoke emanating from the evil-smelling pipe Mackenzie puffed while he was deep in thought.

Suddenly, Mackenzie snapped his fingers loudly. 'Got it!' he cried. 'What we need is a good grass, a copper's nark, and I know just the fella.' He looked very pleased with himself. 'He is at the moment residing in Lincoln prison, but for a spot of remission he will sing like a bloody canary. We'd better start pulling strings.'

'Who is he? Anyone I know?' asked Terry Long with cool sarcasm.

Mackenzie ignored Long's tone. 'He's the biggest rogue who ever set foot in this patch. He was born down here and knows them all. Knuckles O'Leary, they call him. He got his name from the big knuckledusters he wore in the old gang fights.'

'Why are you so sure he will grass?' asked Terry Long. 'I thought there was honour amongst thieves.'

Mackenzie stared aggressively at this polished know-all of an assistant. He was never going to like him. 'Not this bastard,' he growled. 'This one will sing his head off and cough his heart up, he will. He hasn't an ounce of loyalty in him.'

The following Thursday, Joe put the finishing touches to his river scene and packed it up carefully. All being well, he would be able to visit John and Marie on Sunday. But he was not sure about it all being well even now. The situation was growing riskier, he could feel it in his bones. Every day that week there had been plain clothes detectives in the bar, Nelly had informed him during lunch. 'I can spot a copper a mile off,' she boasted. 'Got a nose for coppers, I have.' She sniffed loudly as she attacked the succulent roast beef with the carving knife. 'Believe me, Joe,' she continued, 'it's time to cool off. If I were you, I'd duck out now while I still had the chance.'

Joe sighed. He knew she was right. 'You'll get ten years next time if you're caught,' she warned him. 'And if Mackenzie gets Spinx and Doug, they won't be around to draw their pensions either . . .'

Joe listened quietly as he enjoyed his excellent lunch. Nelly might be a chatterbox but she was still a good cook. She was right, of course, everything she said was right, but how was he to escape from this sticky web of crime? Nowadays he felt that the only way was to leave the country completely. Perhaps he could go out to Australia. Anne's family lived there and he still had that letter that contained the address of her parents. He often thought of Anne now. Nothing had ever replaced the mutual love and respect that they had had for each other. What a pity that he had gone and spoiled what might have developed into a perfect relationship. The passionate Queenie, the sweet naïve Nelly, the charming Marie, all had something to offer in their own way, but thoughts of Anne lived deep down inside him and probably would forever now.

Joe was now fully established as one Joe Abrahams the barman, with a phoney set of work cards. Perhaps it would be wise to let Joe Walowski die, he thought, and disappear forever. Like a hive of buzzing bees, these thoughts harassed him. He was feeling quite agitated, so after lunch he took his sketch-book down to the wall beside the river and sat down to draw swift sketches of the river craft. The first ship he outlined was a cargo vessel flying a Polish flag. It was anchored just outside Tower Bridge, moving gently up and down on the water. Soon peace and tranquillity returned to him and calmed him, just as it always did once his creative instincts were fulfilled. Now he felt ready for the night ahead . . .

Just after midnight, Joe was still sitting in the room watching the green telephone. It seemed to have taken the shape of a frog with a wide grinning mouth. When it suddenly rang, Joe almost jumped out of his skin. He grabbed the receiver and slapped it against his ear. It was Hustler's Pop.

'They got Doug,' the breathless voice said. 'Me and the boss got away. Tell the Queen, the lid's off.' Joe felt giddy. It was all going wrong. What was going to happen? He could feel panic gripping him by the throat. What should he do? Suddenly he heard soft footsteps on the stairs. Then Queenie appeared in the doorway. She looked cool and calm in a scarlet dressing gown. Joe knew that she had been listening in on the extension.

'You got the bad news, Joe?' she asked abruptly.

Joe nodded dumbly.

Queenie walked across the room and rummaged in the desk. 'It's all clean,' she said. 'Sphinx took all the evidence away. Now the money in here is mine.' She stuffed it in her pocket. 'I'll put it with the takings,' she added, 'just in case they question you.'

Her keen eyes scanned the room. 'Now, don't forget, you're Joe Abrahams and you work for me behind the bar. Now, I'd get into bed, if I were you.' With a whiff of perfume, she swept coolly out again.

Joe slipped his braces off and crept into bed where he lay crying and shivering under the blanket until the wail of sirens told him that the police were coming. It all seemed overwhelming – that dreaded sound, those flashing blue lights, that heavy tread upon the stair, the shrill voice of Queenie as she argued with them.

'What's up there?' Joe could hear a gruff voice demanding.

'Nothing,' she said. 'It's just where the barman sleeps.'

Now the noises were inside the room. Joe was hidden under his blanket. Then someone gave him a terrific thump on the back.

'Get up and come out!'

Joe sat up and stared about him in fright. Six policemen were turning his room over, opening the cupboard, pulling out his belongings, climbing up the rafters. Looming over him stood a scarlet-faced man.

'And who are you?' the man demanded.

'Joe Abrahams. I work behind the bar.' The words barely came out of his mouth.

'Been here all night, I presume.' Mackenzie's keen eyes scrutinised him. 'So I suppose you've never heard of Mr Spinx.' His tone was ironic.

Joe shook his head, causing the detective to puff out his cheeks, either in disgust or impatience, it was hard to tell.

'There's nothing here, cleaned it out they have,' said one of the policemen.

'Come on, let's go turn out Billy Douglas's house next,' said Mackenzie. Turning to Joe, he said, 'Get up and go downstairs. I might need you yet.'

Downstairs in the kitchen, two uniformed constables were guarding Beery Bill, who was dressed only in a striped shirt and woolly long johns. He was cussing and swearing having been dragged out from his sleeping quarters below the barrels.

Queenie was there, too. She looked calm but was pale and smoked incessantly while hurling occasional insults at the police. 'I think you've taken a bloody liberty, Mac,' she snarled, 'to raid me without a warning.'

Mackenzie shrugged. 'Well, love, somebody bloody well had to,' he said quietly.

Dawn had come, casting light through the windows, before the police all finally left. Feeling cold and tired, Joe, Queenie and Bill all drank hot coffee laced with brandy. No one spoke, but it was obvious that they were all equally relieved that the visit from the fuzz was over.

On Sunday Joe went to visit John and Marie as promised. The painting he had done for them was wildly praised, and was immediately placed on the wall over the sitting-room fireplace for all their friends and neighbours to see and admire. For Joe it was an extremely pleasant day. John and Marie seemed so extraordinarily happy together that it gave him peace of mind just being part of that little family for the whole day. After a delicious evening meal cooked by Marie, they played Monopoly.

'Oh, lovely!' Marie cried, waving a bundle of toy bank notes. 'How wonderful it would be to have lots of money, and to be able to buy and sell houses like this.'

'Give over, Marie,' joked John. 'We ain't paid for this one yet.'

'I know,' Marie said ruefully, 'but sometimes I wish

we could sell it and move right into the heart of the country.'

'Is that what you would really like, Marie?' asked Joe, watching with interest as those cornflower eyes went all dreamy.

Marie had put her elbows on the table and her chin in her hands. 'Yes, Joe, I'd love to have a big old-fashioned house with lots of space for the children. It's mostly the space I want, but also to get my John away from London.'

Joe understood her deep dread of John's crooked family. He squeezed her hand. 'I sincerely hope you get all you wish for, Marie,' he said.

On the journey home, Joe tried in vain to think of some ways of passing some money to Marie without her knowing how he had come by it. With a little capital behind them life would be less of a struggle for John and Marie. And for John there would no longer be the slightest temptation to fiddle. Marie was obviously having to work hard on him to keep him straight. Yes, life was always a problem. Even in that happy little homestead, the serpent reared its head.

Chapter Eighteen

Knuckles O'Leary

On Monday a new face appeared in the lounge bar at Queenie's Castle. He had flat battered features, a large bull-like head and hard mean eyes surrounded by pockets of loose flesh. He was heavily built and leaned a hefty shoulder against the ornate post that supported the bar. His podgy hands displayed heavy knuckleduster rings.

As Joe made his way quietly through the bar to the kitchen, he thought that the newcomer's face was oddly familiar. He found Nelly already puffed up with indignation like a cockney sparrow deprived of its crust. 'See him?' she cried, as Joe walked in.

'See who, Nelly?' he asked mildly.

'Why that git, Knuckles O'Leary. They've bleedin' gorn and let him out.'

Joe's heart jumped high. So that was *him*. He thought he had recognised him, and that's why the face was familiar. At last he was there, the bullet-headed hooligan who had mown him down all those years before in that alley, and the one who possibly killed young Maisie. At last. So it had not been a waste of time after all. Joe's heart thumped wildly in his chest.

'He's apparently got about six months' remission,' Nelly went on. 'Bloody sauce. Wait till I tell my

old man . . .' But Joe did not reply. Walking over
to the door, he stood and watched this villain, this
man who had been the instigator of that murderous
crime which had given him a long prison sentence.
Just like that proverbial spider he had walked into
the queen's parlour.

Queenie herself seemed distracted at lunch. She ate
very little and the dark geranium colour of her lipstick
made her mouth stand out clearly from her extremely
pallid face. Scrutinising her carefully, Joe suddenly
thought how lovely Queenie must have been in
her early youth, with that marble skin and full
mouth. But, like an exotic flower, she was fading
fast. Her cheeks were now slightly puffy under her
eyes and there were lines on her forehead that the
heavy pancake of make-up could not disguise.

She noticed him staring at her and said abruptly,
'You can take your money from the safe, Joe. Old
Bill won't come back any more. They picked the
place clean like bloody vultures.'

'Anything bothering you?' Joe asked gently.

'Nothing more than usual,' Queenie replied rather
wearily, 'unless you count that stir-crazy fool Knuckles
O'Leary.'

Joe was interested. Queenie was well known for
her home which welcomed ex-cons. What was so
different about this ex-con, he wondered. 'Can I
help?' he said.

'If you can keep that mad dog off my back I'd
be extremely grateful,' replied Queenie. 'But it's not
going to be easy. He's here for a reason and that's
what's worrying me,' explained the Queen.

Over the dishes in the back kitchen, Nelly's face
was scarlet with excitement. She nudged Joe with her
elbow. 'Told yer, didn't I? He's turned copper's nark.
He'd never have got out of the nick otherwise.'

Joe was wondering how he should make contact

with this dreaded villain who seemed to have upset the women in this hive of crime. By now he was convinced that it was this man who held the key to all his troubles. Indeed, those words from the past burned in his brain like fire: 'I'd better run down to Queenie's and tell the Gaffer.' This was the chap who had uttered those words. At the time they had had no meaning but now it was all becoming very clear . . .

Joe watched intently all that evening as Knuckles sidled up close to Queenie as she sat on her high stool. From the venomous glances she shot at the burly man, Joe could tell that she really hated him. Well, that was something, but now Joe found himself wondering how much Queenie knew about Maisie's murder. He had to find out.

And so Joe decided right there to have one last throw of the dice before he cleared off forever. It was time to act.

After a lot of thought, Joe made his way down to the market where he purchased a small tape recorder and two bottles of rather potent brandy. Returning to his room, he hid the tape recorder where no one would see it. He put on his shirt and corduroy trousers, then took his sketch-book down to the public bar where a darts match was in progress. It was very crowded in there, with large groups of beer-swilling lads in overalls, a crowd of women and the regulars who drank enthusiastically as they watched the darts match across the room.

Joe looked around. The only truly familiar face was that of Hustler's Pop, whose little white head seemed to be everywhere at once. Then to his surprise, Joe suddenly caught the sound of his own mother tongue. It was pure Polish. He stared at the knot of sailors in their grey-blue overalls. *They must be the crew of the ship near the bridge*, he thought. They've jumped ashore for an unofficial drink. He then proceeded to sketch them in various poses. One fairly young man noticed him and came over to ask him what he was doing. Joe explained that he was an artist. The sailor spoke very good English and offered to buy Joe a drink. Joe happily sat down with him and the two of them discussed the situation behind the Iron Curtain. The sailor told Joe that he had looked forward to docking in Glasgow but some change of shipping plans had landed them in London. He was not impressed, he said. He told him that he was in love with a Scottish girl he had met on an earlier voyage but could not get the necessary papers to marry her.

Joe was all sympathy. The two men drank vodka and struck up a friendship, this blond mate free from Communist Poland and the artistic off-beat Joe of Polish parents. After several drinks, they sang old folk songs which Joe remembered from his youth. The young sailor had tears in his eyes when he had finished. 'It's for my Scottish lass, I weep,' he said. 'If I could get away I'd jump ship and be on my way up to Glasgow in the morning.'

'Is it impossible?' Joe asked.

The sailor nodded. 'Money is the only thing that makes it possible, but I have none,' he replied gloomily.

'How often do you make this trip?' Joe asked.

'Well, if I sign on again, I'll be back in five weeks.'

Joe pondered for a while. 'How would you like to switch identity with me and get five hundred pounds to start in Scotland?'

The young man stared at him in astonishment. 'Don't joke,' he begged. But Joe solemnly shook his head and offered him his hand. 'Make your plans, I'll meet you here in five weeks. We will switch papers and see if you can get me abroad without anyone knowing.'

'It might be done,' replied the puzzled sailor, 'but I cannot see why you want to do this crazy thing.'

'Never mind about that,' Joe told him. 'Just get things organised. Money is available.'

'It will be dangerous for me,' the young man said. 'You won't let me know now . . .'

'No, now don't forget I'm Joe Abrahams, the barman, if you want to find me.'

Just then, a heavy figure lumbered into the bar creating a disturbance. He was well drunk and slobbering. Knuckles O'Leary had arrived.

As he stood there and glared about him, the atmosphere seemed to change. Several respectable couples got up and left the bar. Knuckles then walked towards Joe.

'Where's all these fucking foreigners come from?' he yelled.

The ship's crew drew close together and nudged each other as though to suggest that it was time they were back on board. They put down their beer glasses and began to leave.

'Piss off!' yelled Knuckles at them, as they filed quietly past. Joe could hear them muttering insults at Knuckles in Polish but they all left peacefully enough. But once the sailors had gone, Knuckles launched into a tirade against all foreigners. With every other word a swear word, he let forth. 'Ship the whole lot of them off, I would,' he shouted. 'There are all our blokes shut up in the nick and the fucking blacks and foreigners are taking over. It's disgusting, that's what I say.'

Nobody took much notice of Knuckles' speech. In fact, the locals seemed anxious to avoid him. But Joe realised that this was his chance. Walking over to Knuckles, he asked him to have a drink. He was amazed at his own courage.

'Who the fucking hell are you?' Knuckles demanded with a scowl.

'I'm Joe. I work in the bar but it's my night off,' replied Joe.

'I'll have a whisky,' said Knuckles, swaying from side to side and clenching his big fists as though he desperately wanted to punch someone.

Hoping that Knuckles would not recognise him, Joe persevered. He was determined to get Knuckles' confidence. So much depended on it.

Now Knuckles was peering at him. 'Where have I seen you before?'

Joe's heart missed a beat, but he need not have worried.

'Been inside, have yer?'

'Yes,' replied Joe, trying to look nonchalant. 'I've done a spell of porridge.'

This answer seemed to placate Knuckles who looked greedily at Joe. 'How are you fixed?' he asked. 'Could do with a tenner till I get on me feet.'

Joe put a finger to his lips. 'Can't talk here,' he said. 'Come upstairs, I've got a drink up there.'

Knuckles looked at him with an evil squint as a lewd expression appeared on that unpleasant face. 'Come upstairs . . .' He repeated the words Joe had spoken. ''Ere, you ain't bent, are yer? Don't want no queer pouncing on me.'

Joe laughed. 'No, I'm not bent. You're quite safe with me. And if you're still interested in conning me for a tenner, you'd better come where we can discuss it. I might be able to put some work your way.'

Knuckles stared back vacantly, as his drunken mind tried hard to remember what it was he was supposed to find out at Queenie's. Then suddenly the penny dropped. 'Right, boss,' he said. 'I'll be up in a minute.'

Joe pointed the way he should go and then discreetly

left the bar. Upstairs in his room, he placed the tape recorder on the top shelf of the cupboard under the sink and switched it on. Then he put out two glasses and the bottle of brandy. Now he could hear Knuckles lumbering heavily up the rickety fire escape.

Joe felt a flutter of excitement as he poured a glass of brandy for Knuckles to gulp down greedily. Joe offered Knuckles Spinx's chair which he had drawn up with its back to the tape recorder. He hoped fervently that the hum of the machine would not be noticed.

Knuckles had settled comfortably in the chair and did not seem bothered. His eye was resting on the bottle and he was ready for a refill. 'Like old times, this is,' he said, looking around appreciatively. 'Used to hang about up here, I did, when I worked for the Gaffer.'

'The Gaffer?' Joe tried to sound as though he had never heard the name before.

'Yeah,' continued Knuckles. 'The Gaffer used to be Jack the Lad about here. And he still is, in the nick.' He sniggered. 'Fancy the Queen myself, I do.'

Joe refilled Knuckles' glass. It was essential to get him in a very talkative mood. He brought out a wad of notes which Knuckles eyed greedily.

'Short of a bit of ready cash, I am,' Knuckles said.

'How much do you want?' Joe asked.

'Make it twenty-five,' said Knuckles. 'I know you're all doing all right. There's a lot of talk about some sparklers gone missing.' He had a sneer on his face as he said this but Joe ignored it and handed him the notes.

The large hand full of cheap heavy rings grabbed it. Joe winced. There was something about this bully that he detested but having managed to get him into a moderately civil mood it would be stupid to back out now. How was he going to get him to talk some more? He racked his brains in desperation, but he need not have worried. The booze was doing the trick. Knuckles now had the bottle beside him and with legs spread widely in front, he leaned back in the chair and talked his head off. He boasted of his boxing days and when he won fights. He told Joe about the time he had done one fellow up, and sliced another's face in half with a razor.

As he rattled on, Joe was thinking what a pity it was that capital punishment had been abolished. A man like this deserved to hang, he thought. Then he remembered that he might have been hanged himself for the Maisie murder. He used to think about that a lot in prison.

Knuckles was now shouting and waving his hands as he ranted on.

'I might have a little job for you later,' Joe said.

'Good,' said Knuckles. 'Yeah, the old boss relied on me. Best muscles man he had, I was, but the bastard grassed on me over that floosie what got done up.'

Quickly Joe refilled his glass. 'That was before my time,' he said quietly, trying not to look excited. Knuckles was only too happy to chatter on.

'Bloody bad, that was,' he continued. 'She was not a bad-looking kid, and I was going to rough her up a bit because she cocked up a job. She fought back like a bleedin' wild cat so I threatened to chiv her. The little bitch kneed me in the balls and I lost me balance. The gun went off and she was hit in the face.'

Joe was shaking as sweat poured from his brow. Then feeling almost sick with apprehension, he prayed for Knuckles to go on and actually mention the name of his victim.

Suddenly, Knuckles had become maudlin. He shook his head and grimaced. 'Upset me, it did. Couldn't believe me own eyes. She wasn't a bad kid, Maisie, but she was a proper little whore. Cocked up the job, she did.'

There it was, the vital piece of evidence! Joe breathed a deep sigh of relief.

But Knuckles still had not finished. 'The Gaffer set some poor sod of a school teacher up for the job and then wanted to get me out of the picture. He ran down that kid's ponce. He was some kid who used to go around on a motorbike and he ran off with the lolly.'

Got it, thought Joe jubilantly. *I've got it all.* Now, how was he to get rid of him? Knuckles was still eyeing the remains of the bottle. 'Take it with you,' said Joe brightly.

Suddenly those mean eyes flashed in a paranoid manner and there was a complete change in Knuckles. 'Trying to get rid of me, are yer?' he demanded. He looked very nasty.

Joe shrugged. 'Well, I'd like to be up early tomorrow,' he explained.

'I bet the Queen's in bed,' Knuckles slurred suddenly. 'She'll be just the job for a bit of the other.' He made an obscene gesture causing Joe to shudder inwardly. 'I think she fancies me.' Knuckles leered horribly. 'I might just pay her a visit.' The Irishman staggered to his feet swaying.

Joe was not quite sure what to do. He ought to try to stop him going to Queenie's room but Joe's main concern was how to get out the tape which now had this vital evidence recorded on it.

Knuckles had taken off his smart jacket and was folding it neatly on the bed. 'I can't kip in that,' he said in a slurred voice, 'I only got it today. Cost me thirty quid, it did.' Unsteadily, he made for the door.

Joe stepped in front of him. 'Not that way,' he said. 'You will wake up the whole house.'

But Knuckles snarled and pushed Joe violently to one side. 'The Queen won't mind me waking her,' he muttered, and before Joe could gather his wits, Knuckles was on his way down to Queenie's bedroom. Joe dashed to the sink to switch off the tape recorder and pull out the plug. *No doubt Queenie can look after herself*, he thought.

Suddenly from below came an ear-splitting scream, followed by the smashing of glass. There was a terrific thump and then silence.

Grabbing the nearest weapon he could see, his pallet knife, Joe dashed downstairs to rescue Queenie. He rushed into her bedroom to find her standing by her bed looking terribly distraught. Her golden hair was hanging loose around her shoulders and she was wearing a very short nylon nightdress. She was holding her hand to her face and staring dumbly in the direction of Knuckles O'Leary who was lying stretched out where he had fallen. His huge head was resting in the fireplace, and his forehead was bleeding profusely. At his feet lay the large brass lamp, now all bent, which Queenie had aimed at him.

'Jesus Christ!' muttered Joe as he looked down at Knuckles' open mouth and eyes turned up in his head.

'Whoever let that bastard in?' screamed Queenie, suddenly finding her voice.

'What happened?' asked Joe innocently. Kneeling down next to Knuckles' body, he raised him slightly. The head flopped back into a grotesque position and thick dark blood flowed out of the back of his head where he had crashed onto the brass fire dogs as the lamp struck his forehead. 'I think he's dead,' Joe said flatly.

Queenie stared at Knuckles in disbelief. Then she said coldly, 'Go and get Beery Bill and Hustler's Pop to help move him out of here.'

Joe was impressed by her calm manner. How quickly she had recovered from what must have been a terrible fright. Already she was ready to act in this emergency.

Within ten minutes Beery Bill and Hustler's Pop were carrying Knuckles' heavy body down the stairs to the cellar where it would be hidden until they decided how to dispose of it.

Feeling as though this was all unreal, or part of a bad dream, Joe crept back up the stairs to bed. He was feeling cold and shivery, but as he passed Queenie's door he could hear her heartbroken weeping.

He opened the door quietly and stood in the doorway. 'Don't cry, Queenie,' he said gently. He went over and held her tight, cuddling her as he might have cuddled a distressed child. 'Don't worry, it will sort itself out,' he murmured.

'But who let him in, Joe?' Queenie sobbed. 'I've always been afraid of him. I know what he is capable of.'

'I don't know,' he lied. 'But never mind, love, try not to worry.' Thus Joe consoled her.

'Don't go, Joe,' she said. 'Don't leave me alone tonight.' She held him to her tight.

An hour later, they were still in a passionate embrace. So the living went on living and the dead lay down in the dark cellar.

Chapter Nineteen

Clearing Up

The next day it had to be business as usual at Queenie's Castle. Everyone went about their tasks and said nothing while Knuckles O'Leary continued to lie in the dark beer cellar covered with a sack.

As Joe set about his jobs in the kitchen, he shuddered to recall how he had held onto O'Leary's legs while Hustler's Pop and Beery Bill had carried the other end. He could still see the dark blood frothing from the wide open mouth. It had been quite a night. After the body had been disposed of, he found himself in bed with Queenie. She had cried non-stop and then been so passionate. Why, she seemed to have been driven by self-pity, but she had forced Joe to make love to her continuously.

Joe felt desperate now. He was again involved in another murder. Should the police get him, he would not see the outside world for quite a while. It had been an accident and partly his own fault, so early that morning he had tried to persuade Queenie to call the police and tell them Knuckles had broken into the premises and tried to rape her. But Queenie was having none of it. Clad in her dressing gown, drinking gin and swallowing tranquillisers all at the same time, she said, 'Don't be such a fool, Joe. Can't you imagine what it would be like? Why, those cops would never stop until they had dragged out every detail. What a heyday the Sunday papers would have then! No, Joe, I would be finished, and I swear they will never shut *me* up in prison. I'd do myself in before they did that, I've always said I would.'

Joe nodded. He knew she was right, so he said nothing more but sat with his shoulders hunched wondering how he was going to come out of all this.

'I've sent a word to the Gaffer,' Queenie said. 'He'll know what's best to do.'

Word came back from the Gaffer that afternoon. Queenie gave them all the orders and Joe obeyed, along with the others. Without any emotion, Joe helped to strip the clothes off Knuckles' large and flabby body. Then they bundled him up in a sack and sewed it tight with a large sacking needle. Beery Bill made a real professional job of it. 'This is just like when we used to bury our mates at sea,' he told them proudly, thinking back to his sailor days during the war.

At last the body was all trussed up and tied to a plank which had a heavy weight attached to it. In the dead of that night, Pickles took Hustler's Pop and a very drunk Beery Bill to help push the body out to sea.

Joe stayed behind.

'Stay with me, Joe,' pleaded Queenie. She looked surprisingly scared. It was not like her to be shaken by anything, but this business of Knuckles had really shocked her. He peered through the window as the other men hoisted the bundle up from the cellar. Two wooden flaps opened up in the back yard and the body was hoisted up on rope by a very cheerful Pickles. He might have been handling a barrel of beer for all he seemed to care.

Joe watched the bundle being shoved into a van

with mixed feelings. He was both terrified and desperate to laugh. The whole experience seemed so unreal.

Once the old van had roared out of the yard, Queenie seemed more relaxed. She swallowed some sleeping pills and washed them down. 'I'm going to bed, Joe, and this time I'd advise you to do the same.'

So, for the first time in two days, Joe returned to his rooms. He was desperately tired and very confused. With a great sigh, he sat down on the bed and sat still for a few moments. Suddenly, to his horror, he saw Knuckles' jacket hanging on the back of the chair. What a giveaway! If anyone had seen it, they would have known it was Joe who had let Knuckles in. He had to get rid of it! Feeling apprehensive, he grabbed the jacket and fumbled about in the cupboard until he had found a piece of brown paper and string. He tied the jacket up in a neat parcel and stared about the room. What was he going to do with it? It was still night – about half past two in the morning. Staring out of the window, he looked down at the cold green river as it flowed swiftly past at full tide. Then he had an idea. He would throw the bundle into the river. Once it was waterlogged it would sink to the bottom. Pushing the little window wide open, he leaned out and threw the parcel down with all his might. He heard the splash as it entered the water and then all he could hear was the rush of the tide.

Good, he had got rid of that dangerous evidence. No one would know that Knuckles had been in his room. He felt more at ease but he was still very unhappy about what had happened. Now that Knuckles was dead it was going to be harder to clear his name. The precious tape was pretty much useless. It could not be used to clear him if Knuckles was not around to be found guilty. What a mess! Wearily, he got undressed, climbed into bed and slept soundly until morning.

While Joe slept so soundly, the river tide receded, leaving the parcel lying on the muddy bank, drying out in the morning sun.

Along the muddy shore came an old man, a scavenger with a bent back and a pair of wellington boots. He was a well-known character in those parts, combing the foreshore for bits and pieces left by the tide. He made quite a good living from the debris the river threw up – the most unusual things could end up in the water to be recycled by him. The man spotted the parcel and undid it. Shaking out the rumpled jacket, he inspected it carefully. 'Good stuff,' he muttered. 'Might get a bit for it.' With that, he rammed it into the pram to join the old iron and empty bottles he had collected that morning. 'It'll fetch a few bob, that will,' the scavenger repeated to himself as he squelched his dilapidated way through the river mud.

Chapter Twenty

Another Death

Two days later, Joe returned to his rooms after lunch to find Spud sitting in the office with a very sorrowful expression on his face. He was sitting very still and was dressed in a dark blue sweater and grey trousers. Between his knees he had a navy holdall with a leather strap and zip along the top.

'Hello, Spud,' Joe greeted him warmly. 'I'm glad you're back safe.'

Spud did not reply immediately but he kept looking at the floor. Joe noticed that his eyes were red as though from weeping, but he thought that it was probably from the wind or the salt spray from the sea as he brought his boat across the Channel.

Spud suddenly looked up. 'I've got a great shock for you, Yossel. The boss is dead.'

Joe stared back at him in amazement. Who was dead? Spinx? It was incredible. 'You're joking,' he said, 'you're kidding me.'

Spud shook his head. 'It's not a joke,' he said. 'It happened last night. He just went out like a light. He was sorting out the money to pay the boys off. He was sitting at his desk, and then he went, peacefully, like he was asleep. I had called at his house as he had asked me to, and his wife asked me to get him to come down from his study for tea. God, the shock it gave me! I went in and said, "It's me, boss," but he didn't answer. When I got close I knew something was wrong. He was lying back as if he were asleep, but I knew he was a goner, Yos. We had it a bit rough on that last trip, and he was worried over Doug. We humped them damned sparklers half-way across the Continent, they was so hot we could not get rid of them easily.'

Joe was still trying to absorb the news that Spinx was dead. Why, he had been larger than life and so healthy looking. Well, he had said that he was going to get out, and fate had decided he should go out forever.

Tears had begun to trickle down Spud's rough cheek. He wiped them away with the back of his hand. 'I'm sorry, Yos, I just can't help it. We'd been friends since our days in the army.'

Joe patted his shoulder sympathetically. 'Does anyone else know?' Joe asked.

'No, I came to tell you first. The boss had got trust in you, Yossel. He was sorting out the lolly from the last job when he popped off, so I brought it all up. I brought all his papers, as well. Even his missus didn't know his business. There's twelve thousand pounds in here to share out amongst the lads. I got my cut and Spinx took his. The rest is for you and the lads.' He handed the navy holdall to Joe. 'Perhaps you could get rid of any papers that might be dodgy, will you, Joe?'

Joe smiled and nodded. 'Of course I will,' he said.

Spud shook his head again thoughtfully. 'I wonder if he had some kind of premonition because before we left on the last trip he wrote a letter to his wife, saying that if anything happened to him he was to be brought home and buried from his own little house on the street. He was born there and he still owned it. That blind fella rents it. Anyway, Spinx wanted to be laid to rest in Manor Park cemetery where his parents are buried. And it's a funny request, isn't it? Spinx was a well-respected farmer down where I live. He had a lot of property there, yet he wants to be buried back here in the East End.' Spud's voice sounded choked. 'You know,' he said brokenly, 'the boss dotted his i's and crossed his t's to the very last. Everything was put in order, all written down, and then he just went peacefully to sleep. Anyway, I've brought it all over to you, Yossel. I didn't want no stranger poking through it. Spinx was known as a very respectable citizen in that village, and I didn't want to spoil things for his wife. He trusted you, Yossel, and you've got the head for these things. So do us a favour, mate, take over.'

With tears rolling, he pointed to the battered hold-all. 'It's all there, Yos, in separate envelopes. He was getting it all ready for the pay-off. I just can't believe he's gone. We've been together for so many years.'

Joe knew that there was no consolation for Spud. Only time would be able to take away the hurt of the loss of his boss. Opening the bag, he rummaged through its contents – the old ledgers, the bills of sale, envelopes with bank notes inside. To the end, Spinx had kept his affairs in order. He felt at a loss. With the tape now useless and himself an accessory to murder, he was in even more of a mess than before. Perhaps he was hoping that something in the bag would help him, but there seemed to be little of such importance there. Spinx had left nothing to chance, not even an address or telephone number.

Joe looked at the bulky envelopes. Each had the nickname of a gang member written on the front. Inside was the carefully divided money.

'We had a very rough coming back across the Channel last time,' said Spud. 'It wasn't at all easy to shift those sparklers, and I don't think all that worry can have done him a lot of good.'

Joe tore up the ledger and burnt it page by page over the small spirit stove.

Spud got to his feet. 'Well, I'm blowing now. Me boat's on the slipway, and I don't want Old Bill clambering all over it. I'll be up for the funeral, see you then.'

Joe was examining the tightly packed envelopes in the bag. 'Get rid of them quick, Yos,' he warned. With that, he left, that stocky little loyal sailor who had come to the end of his life of crime.

At midnight after the bar had closed, the rest of the boys gathered in the office. That red-headed giant Pickles was still covered in oil, Hustler, wearing his immaculate white roll-necked jumper, looked pale and worried, while the long-haired photographer, Flash, was very subdued for once. Looking at them, Joe was suddenly aware of how very attached to these boys he had become. There was Beery Bill still breathing and wheezing alcohol fumes and Hustler's Pop looking very dapper and clean.

Earlier in the day, Hustler had left his corner to round up the younger lads from their various haunts of vice to inform them of the death of their boss, and to tell them that there was a meeting at Queenie's when the bar was closed.

Joe opened his own envelope. Two thousand pounds was his cut! He had never had such a fortune! he smiled wryly. The irony of this scene was that he would probably not be around to spend this money anyway, if things went according to plan . . . Joe began to think about John and Marie. How he would like to help them, he thought.

Queenie was sitting in the corner looking quite shattered by Spinx's death but she took her own cut in a cold nonchalant manner.

'We're getting out, Yossel,' said the young lads as
he gave them Snatcher's cut to take to him. 'We're all
going to Las Vegas for a long holiday. It's just got too
hot down here.'

'Good luck, boys,' said Joe. There was an extra
packet for Doug's Irish colleen, Bernadette. Hustler's
Pop took charge of that, and there was a smaller
packet for Beery Bill. At last, the pay-off was over
and they all went their own way. It was the break up
of the gang and Joe was not sorry, but in his bones
he knew he was not yet free. And the creepiest thing
of all was that nothing was said about Knuckles at all.
It was as if he had never existed.

Chapter Twenty-One

A Puzzled Cop

Superintendent Mackenzie was feeling rather annoyed
and disconcerted. It was three weeks since he had
negotiated to get Knuckles O'Leary paroled, and he
had heard nothing since then. The man had been out
for a while now but nothing had been seen or heard of
him since his initial briefing. As a copper's nark he had
therefore been useless, particularly as he could not be
found. Reading the reports, Mackenzie's annoyance
began to turn into worry. His men had searched the
gambling houses and billiard halls during the day and
vice slots and gambling clubs at night.

Every East End club had been thoroughly combed
but there had not been sight or sound of O'Leary. It
was all very puzzling. And since he never even paid
one of his weekly visits to his parole officer, a warrant
was out for O'Leary's arrest. The only information
they had to go by was from a old lady he used to lodge
with. She had told the police that O'Leary had gone
back there, and had left a few articles of property, but,
she said, he had gone to get a new suit at Sam Levy's
in Whitechapel and had not returned.

With a growing frown on his brow, Mackenzie
perused the reports. There was not much to go
on here. Surely O'Leary would not have gone on
the run. He had no money and very few friends.

Mackenzie shook his head. No, it was not their way.
No, O'Leary would hang about down the East End.
Criminals seldom changed their ways, like the old
London pigeons they always went home to roost.

'Any more news from the grapevine?' he asked
Terry Long who had just come into his office.

Terry nodded. He looked rather pleased with
himself. 'Yes, Mac, I've got several items and one
will surprise you.'

'Let's have it, then,' growled Mackenzie.

'Well, it seems that three weeks back Knuckles
visited an East End tailor. He left his old togs with
the tailor and went off wearing the new suit. He
never came back, and the tailor says he's still owed
twenty quid.'

'That's funny,' muttered Mackenzie, 'very funny.
They like to look smart, these boys, they don't usually
knock a good tailor.'

'Also, I'm afraid your old friend Spinx has snuffed
it,' added Terry.

The superintendent looked surprised. 'Well, I'm
blowed,' he declared. 'How'd it happen?'

'He just popped off peacefully sitting at his desk. He
wasn't in London, but in some country village where
he lived for quite a while.'

Mackenzie nodded thoughtfully. 'Well, that's also
a surprise. Never thought he'd die a natural death,'
he said.

Terry continued, delighted that he knew things the
super didn't. 'It seems he's about to be buried from his
old house in this area, this week sometime. The traffic
cops have had information of a big funeral procession.
Seems like it will be a big affair.'

'I know the place,' said Mackenzie. 'Next door to
Billy Douglas in Stern Street. Born and brought up
there, he was. An old blind man has been living in that
house for a long time. I didn't know it still belonged

to Jim Spinx. They all started out down there, nicking carrots on the way home from school.'

The younger detective gave a supercilious sneer. 'There goes old Mac,' he muttered, 'back to the good old days.'

But Mac bellowed out, 'Order some bloody flowers. We'll all go to Jimmy Spinx's funeral.'

'Go to the funeral?' Terry Long looked at him askance.

'Don't bloody argue with me, lad,' roared Mackenzie. 'Find out exactly what day the funeral is, because if Knuckles O'Leary is still alive he'll be there for the free beer. If he's not there, we'd better start looking for his body.'

As the two policemen had this conversation, Joe was eating his lunch with Queenie and Nelly in the kitchen of Queenie's Castle. Queenie was looking very thoughtful and solemn.

'I think I'll close the bar on the day of the funeral, out of respect for poor old Spinx,' she said.

Nelly smiled and gave Joe a nudge. 'Don't suppose he'll be getting any more whisky where he's gone.'

Queenie was not amused. She gave Nelly a sorrowful look. 'You'll be paid for the day off, Nelly, if that's what's bothering you,' she retorted sharply. Getting up, she left for her afternoon siesta.

'She's got 'em, ain't she?' exclaimed Nelly, banging the pots and pans around in her usual manner.

'She's got a lot on her mind, Nelly.' Joe valiantly defended Queenie.

Nelly sniffed. 'A lot of darned pills inside her, that's what she's got. Pills to make her sleep, pills to keep her awake, pills to stop her getting in the family way. It's a wonder she don't rattle as she walks, but I suppose they're too wet from all those bottles of gin she pours down on top of them.' Looking quite indignant, Nelly pushed her arms into her old cardigan and marched off home.

Watching her storm out and slam the door, Joe burst out laughing. She was like a funny little bantam hen, was Nelly, her feathers all awry.

Joe quietly finished washing the dishes. Now, to add to the troubles at Queenie's Castle, there was a domestic mutiny on their hands. As he soaped and rinsed the plates he thought about the upcoming funeral. It should be interesting, if nothing else. So far, the police had not been to call, so he was growing increasingly optimistic about making his escape on that Polish ship. He had three more weeks to wait for that. He just had to hope that nothing caught up with him before then. Then these six months living at Queenie's Castle would seem like a strange dream and nothing more, but a very strange one indeed.

Chapter Twenty-Two

The Funeral of a Thief

Spinx's demise had been the topic of conversation in numerous prisons and there were many collections made for floral tributes to a popular old acquaintance. The hard granite face was going to be missed. He was well loved, having given many a helping hand to the other lads financially and otherwise.

Now Spinx lay at peace in that little front parlour where he had been born, mourned by the neighbours as well as the criminal fraternity. Flowers were everywhere, on every table and counter in vases, and wreaths were stacked high along the narrow passage-way out into the street. A lighted candle burned on the coffin as a long-frocked Roman Catholic priest sprinkled holy water and muttered prayers for the soul of this great sinner.

The locals began to line the street to watch the procession as the mourners arrived. One after another, anxious men and women went to pay their last respects to this great man.

Across the road, the plain-clothed policemen watched the house. Mackenzie stood way back but his sharp eyes took in everyone and everything.

Joe arrived as Queenie's escort. She was wearing a dark suit and a little bonnet which sat on the back of her blonde curls and gave her a child-like appearance.

At the sight of that polished coffin, she gave Joe's hand a convulsive clutch and her knees suddenly seemed to go under her. Covering her hands over her face, she wept profusely.

Joe watched her with interest, remembering how little emotion she had shown the week before when the body of Knuckles lay in her room. Well, he would never really understand these people. Under that hard, tough image, they were all soft and very emotional.

A long convoy of cars progressed slowly through the narrow street, gleaming Daimlers, sleek Jaguars, carrying smooth cigar-smoking villains who lived on the spoils of crime, old bangers, and even a van packed tight with slick young men whose pockets bulged with knives, coshes and shooters. There were brown skins and Asian features as the Indian community also paid their respects to Spinx. The traffic to the East End was held up for miles.

Superintendent Mackenzie stood on the kerb, hat in hand, his men beside him. His keen eyes scanned the cars as he watched out for the battered face of Knuckles O'Leary. 'Look at the buggers,' he growled. 'Can't never find them when you want them, and on an occasion like this, they all come out like bugs from the woodwork. And there's very little we can do about it.'

'There's no sign of your grass,' muttered Terry Long.

'No, and that's very odd,' grumbled Mackenzie. 'We'd better put out an all-out alert. They done him in sure as eggs is eggs.'

Mackenzie gave a quick smile of recognition to the sad little Queenie as she passed. But as his eyes settled on Joe sitting beside her, they narrowed.

'Who's that tall bloke escorting the Queen?' he asked.

'That's the new barman and bedmate at Queenie's Castle,' Terry informed him.

'Has he got form?' asked Mackenzie.

'Nothing so far as we know. His name is Joe Abrahams, he's half Jewish, he is. They call him Yossel.'

'Well you'd better go and look some more,' snapped Mackenzie. 'I suspect he's got form as long as his arm, otherwise he wouldn't be hob-nobbing with the Queen.' Mackenzie pushed his way out of the crowd. 'Come on, let's get down to that rogue's gallery. I've seen him before – I'll bet my old shirt on that.'

Later that day, Superintendent Mackenzie stood at the end of a draughty Thames pier. His coat collar was pulled up, and his hands were pushed deep in his pockets, against the chill wind which had turned his bulbous nose almost purple. He was feeling quite cold and hungry but he did not want to leave the spot where he stood because there was a drama going on below. Out in the river was being hauled a waterlogged body that had been discovered deep in the grey mud of the estuary. He was pretty certain whose body it was.

Once the news had reached the police station, Mackenzie had shot out like a bullet from a gun. The river police had picked him up and carried him swiftly in their launch with lights flashing and sirens wailing all the way to the spot where the body had been found.

The body was now loaded up in a black van and Mackenzie was taken to the mortuary where he hung about waiting for the body to be identified.

Sure enough, it was Knuckles O'Leary. There were no articles of clothing, but an operational scar done while in prison, and dental records, also helped them to identify him. And the cause of his death was no mystery. This villain had certainly met his end by foul play. He had been hit on the head with a blunt instrument. But how the man had got into that river, Mackenzie had to find out. And he was pretty sure that something had happened at Queenie's Castle. That, at least, was where his investigation would begin.

At lunchtime the bar was agog with the news of Knuckles' death.

'I knew someone would do that bleeder in before long,' declared Nelly. 'He didn't have many friends, that man, he didn't.'

Sitting high on her stool, Queenie showed not the slightest emotion or even interest in the gossip. Nonchalantly she waved that jewelled hand about as she discussed the weather with her lunchtime customers. Even the most astute of shipping clerks would not have guessed that a curtain was about to come up for the final scene.

Joe spent most of that day peering out of the window at the river, his eyes searching for a sight of the small cargo ship with blue funnels. He was feeling quite frustrated since so far there had been no indication that his saviour, the young Polish sailor, was coming back at all.

Down the road in the market, Old Harry ran a secondhand clothes stall. He had been there for quite a number of years and was a well-known character in the area. That morning Harry was very worried. He did not know what to do. You had to be so careful down this area, where the locals took a poor view of those who ran to Old Bill with every tittle-tattle. But he felt he had to do something.

Harry's concern was over a certain mohair jacket that was hanging up on his stall with a price tag of ten bob. He wished his wife would not keep on nagging about it, but she would not stop. Harry supposed she was right, but what on earth could he do without involving himself? He had bought it in good faith for five bob from the old river scavenger.

'Told yer so,' his wife nagged him now. 'It's here in the paper, a bloke's been done in. You'd better take it up the station.' With a sigh, Harry took down the jacket. He knew she was right, but he was scared out of his wits.

Mackenzie took a walk down to the river, to the spot where Knuckles' jacket had been found. Pensively, he watched as the river washed over his shoes. He looked up at Queenie's Castle and at that old weather vane with its ship and castle which had been a landmark for river travellers for many years. Then his gaze wandered to that small lattice attic window high up in the gables. He took in the barman's attic room with its rickety fire escape which led down to that old unused jetty and gradually incidents which had been quite obscure suddenly became clearer to him. Yes, it was almost time to raid the Queen's castle once more. And this time there would be better results. As he set off for the police station to get the necessary warrants, he muttered to himself, 'I'll have them villains out of there for the last time. And the Queen will run no more bloody bars in London while I'm on the force.'

Chapter Twenty-Three

The Mystery Solved

The news that O'Leary's body had been found alarmed the inhabitants of Queenie's Castle. Beery Bill lay in an alcoholic swoon down in the cellar and as Joe watched out for the ship, Queenie swallowed her tranquillisers. Only wiry little Hustler's Pop remained unperturbed. He just stood in his place on the corner rolling his everlasting thin fag.

'Scarper if you want,' he remarked to Joe. 'After all, you were never really one of us. If Old Bill gets me it will be for a lot more than disposing of old Knuckles.' He gave a little titter. 'Done the bloody dustman out of a job, I have.'

Joe was amused at the man's humour but he was very anxious. That moment had almost arrived, and he had quite mixed feelings about leaving. He would be sad to go and he would miss the happy friends he had found in this waterside tavern. But while he was not yet sure if he would be leaving on the ship or in a Black Maria, he could relax.

'I'm rather concerned about the Queen,' he said to Hustler's Pop.

The old man looked at him reassuringly. 'Don't worry,' he said. 'I'll stick by the missus if no one else does. The old Gaffer has blotted his copy book, and now they've got him in the security nick. There's been a lot of trouble down here.' His mouth gave an ironic twist. 'Rounded up all the best screws, they have.'

Joe felt worse than ever before. Now Queenie was really alone, a prisoner in her own castle. He felt so sorry for her, and a nagging voice kept telling him that it was his fault. He had, after all, let Knuckles in to the inner sanctum of Queenie's Castle. He wanted to stay to look after her but he was also desperate to escape from this place. He had no intention of spending the rest of his life in prison.

Since Spinx's death Queenie had been unusually pathetic and clingy. There were dark rings under her eyes and a sullen droop to her red mouth. Joe's heart went out to her.

Meanwhile, business in the bar continued as usual. Drinks and meals were served, and opening and closing times came around with regularity.

'This place is lousy with coppers, Joe,' Nelly commented one day. 'And they're plain-clothes ones. I don't like those. Getting ready to pounce, they are,' she warned. Her words made Joe shudder, but he felt unable to act, as he still had not made contact with his Polish friend.

Each night as he passed by Queenie's bedroom door, she put out a hand to him. 'Don't leave me alone, Joe,' she begged.

Joe would go in rather reluctantly. Sometimes they made love, while other nights they just sat chatting over a drink until the pills she had taken took effect. Then Joe tucked her up in bed like a small child and went upstairs to his lonely room. From there he would gaze out over the moonlit river which looked cold and dark, reflecting the shore lights in its olive depths. He would get sudden flights of fancy in which he saw Knuckles' body, heavily swollen, floating back up the river like a ship. How he longed for the sight of that Polish flag and the cargo ship with the blue funnels.

Meanwhile, he had begun to take care of the problem of his illicit wealth. He had two thousand, five hundred pounds. It was not a fortune but would be enough to survive for a while. But if the police came they would confiscate it, and if he ended up in prison he would not be able to spend it anyway. He decided that it would be better to lose it or, better still, give it to someone who would make good use of it. He knew already that he would give it to John and Marie but it had to be done without them knowing that it was obtained this dishonestly.

Carefully, he packed up the book of sketches which he had compiled during his months at Queenie's Castle, sketches of London's low life, blowsy middle-aged tipplers from the Jug and Bottle Bar, long-nosed, flat-capped darts players, those faded old lady pianists in their unbecoming hats. There were pictures of the market, the flamboyant stall-holders, fish porters, and crooks galore. He had captured the whole hurly-burly of life down by the riverside. He would present this sketch-book to Marie, for he knew she would appreciate it.

In the centre pages, he placed a wad of notes and then pasted them together. Then he parcelled it up neatly and wrote Marie a farewell letter explaining that he would be gone on her birthday which was at the end of the month so he was sending her her present now. But she was not to open her present until the right time.

Marie cared about doing things right so he knew she would wait until her birthday before opening it. He also bought a sailor's body belt, and filled each waterproof pocket with notes and stitched them up. Kept safe about his waist, that money would see him on his way. He put some money aside to give to Nelly and some for the sailor if he did return. The rest he was going to give to John.

He felt relieved at having sorted out these financial arrangements. If the police came he planned to jump from the fire escape and take his chance down the river. He had no desire to remain cooped up again as a guest of Her Majesty.

Queenie seemed in slightly better spirits that evening when Joe dropped in to see her in her bedroom. She was brushing her fine hair in front of the dressing-table mirror and making herself beautiful for bed. Joe stood hesitantly behind her.

'What's on your mind, Joe?' she asked bluntly.

'I'm going to make a run for it,' he said quietly. His eyes met hers in the mirror.

Queenie's pallid face seemed to turn paler. 'And leave me holding the baby,' she retorted sarcastically.

Joe held her shoulders and squeezed them gently. 'I just think that if the police find out I'm living here they'll come for me sooner or later. And seeing as I've already been convicted of murder, it won't be hard to lay the blame for Knuckles' death on me. That would let you off the hook, Queenie, and give me time to get out of the country.'

The effect of his words was remarkable. Queenie suddenly started to laugh. Joe realised that he had never heard her really laugh before. It was a high-pitched and hysterical laugh, which astonished him. Then she turned to face him, her eyes blazing. She was barely in control of herself and she nearly choked as she said, 'You know, Joe, at times you are ridiculous. I already helped to set you up for young Maisie's murder and here you are begging me to do it again.' She collapsed into peals of laughter.

Joe's jaw dropped. It was what he had suspected but not really dared believe was true. The gorge rose in his throat, making him want to grab her throat and throttle her. She had done all that. She had implicated him in the murder, got him sent to prison, ruined his career forever, and here she was laughing about it. He stood clenching and unclenching his hands, unable to speak.

Now she had take control of herself and her soft voice spoke once more in that sweet cajoling manner. 'Don't get upset about it, Joe, we have had some good times together.'

Joe was feeling quite nauseous, and began to back away from her.

Queenie smirked. 'Yes,' she said. 'When Knuckles came back that night to tell us that Maisie and Nosher had cocked up the job – they had got you involved instead of the bloke who was supposed to be delivering some dope – I was furious. It was me who told Knuckles to rough them both up, as punishment for their incompetence, and in the case of Maisie, as punishment for going with my man . . . She'd slept with the Gaffer some time before.'

Joe recalled Nelly's comments about Queenie's jealousy, as Queenie continued, 'Of course, I didn't exactly tell Knuckles to do her in, but I can't say I was sorry that he did. It was the Gaffer who had the idea to fix you up with the crime. He made sure that Fred the café owner told the police he'd seen you, and that the taxi driver came forward with information. Helping the police is not normally encouraged around here, but in this case it was convenient.'

'So I got rid of Maisie, and the Gaffer made up to me for his sins by making sure nothing came back to me . . .' Queenie chuckled with satisfaction.

Joe stared at her in horror.

'Now, run if you want, Joe,' Queenie said coolly, 'I'll not get in your way.'

Joe glared at her contemptuously and then walked out of her room. So she had always known who he was, she had known about him all the time. She and that damned rogue the Gaffer had trapped him and used him. Now his fury knew no bounds. From now on, it was nothing but his own survival that mattered.

Taking Marie's parcel, he went to find young John at Billingsgate. He knew John would be delivering fish to the market. It was past midnight and the streets were deserted. Joe felt quite spooked and kept looking over his shoulder to see if the police were following him. All sorts of niggly little worries crowded in his head.

He found John where they had been before. John looked as cheerful as ever. 'What's up, mate? Looks like you've been out on the tiles all night,' he said.

'I've come to say goodbye,' replied Joe. 'I'm leaving England, going walkabout. I'm getting too restless. I need to get a bit of colour in my paintings.'

'Lucky sod,' remarked John. 'It's only the likes of us working lads who have to stay put.'

'I've brought a birthday present for Marie,' said Joe. 'Don't let her have it until the end of the month.'

'That's nice of you, but Marie would want to say goodbye, Joe,' said John.

'I'll be gone by the weekend,' said Joe mournfully.

'Well, cheer up,' replied John. 'Anyone would think you was going to be hanged instead of taking a holiday,' he joked.

Chapter Twenty-Four

Escape at Last

The next day, hope came at last. When Joe peered out of the window that morning, he could see, through the river mist which hung like curtains over Tower Bridge, the two blue funnels and limp Polish flag fluttering in the early morning breeze. At last! The ship had returned.

The day passed very slowly as Joe kept up a constant vigil, always looking out of that small lattice window for some sight of the sailor. He could do nothing until he saw him. He felt very excited at the prospect of making his escape.

In the afternoon, he passed Queenie's room again and peered in. Queenie lay on her bed taking her afternoon siesta in a scarlet house coat. Her hair was neatly tied up in a net boudoir cap so that it would not be out of place when she made her evening début. On the bedside table sat the inevitable pills and the gin that never seemed to intoxicate her. Queenie was sleeping a deep drugged sleep but even then she wept. Tiny black lines of mascara trickled down her cheeks.

In spite of himself, Joe crept over to her side and stared at this sad sleeping beauty. For a moment, he wanted to reach out and strangle her, but then, leaning over her, he bent down and kissed her full red lips. Then he left and went upstairs, his own eyes brimming with salty tears. He was confused – he no longer knew what he felt about her.

As he walked upstairs to make his final preparations, he suddenly realised that in all those years of prison and all these weeks here at Queenie's Castle, he had never met the Gaffer, the person responsible for everything that had happened to Joe, to Queenie, and to most of these people he had met here. Well, he wasn't sorry, he thought, and he wasn't sorry that now he probably never would either. Now that he knew who had framed him and why, he felt liberated, and free at last to strike out again on his own and make something of his life.

By five o'clock, just as Joe was beginning to lose heart, he suddenly saw a lonely boat rowing ashore. A slim tall figure tied it to the side and stood looking up at his window. Joe opened the window and signalled for him to climb the fire escape.

Once he had arrived, the young man looked about him nervously. 'I have to be careful,' he said.

'There's no one here,' said Joe reassuringly.

'What's your plan? Is the money still all right?' the sailor asked anxiously.

'Nothing's changed,' Joe replied flatly.

'Well, I must take the money back with me, Joe, because I've promised to sweeten the first engineer and the cook. The others won't be bothered. They probably won't even notice.' He laughed.

'That's quite okay by me,' replied Joe. 'I trust you. Here is the money and here are my identity papers, an insurance card and a couple of phoney references. Those will help you get a job, and that's the best I can do.'

'Good, good,' replied the sailor. 'Once I get to

Scotland they will have a job to dig me out,' he said confidently. 'I'm sick to death of the sea and nothing would set me living in Communist Poland any more.'

Joe heaved a sigh of relief as the sailor continued. 'Well, that's settled. I'll hand you my seaman's papers, and then this is the plan: I've brought you a pair of overalls.' He handed Joe the faded grey-blue boilersuit which he had been wearing when they first met. 'Put these on at about nine o'clock and then mingle with the boys in the bar. We'll be jumping ship to come to the bar at that time. It's all laid on, and the ship sails again before midnight. You must go back to it with the boys. Well, good luck, Joe, I've got to go in case I am missed.'

Joe took his hand and shook it firmly. 'Good luck to you, boy, and to your bonnie lass in Glasgow,' he said jubilantly.

The plan had been finalised. He could not believe his good luck. In just two or three hours, this nightmare would be over.

Now he could hear Queenie moving about down below. She seemed to be pacing the floor like a caged lioness. He knew he would miss her despite everything.

When the sailor had gone, Joe trimmed his hair very short and wriggled into the washed out oily overalls. Joe Walowski was about to die and Jan Rudski, Polish seaman, was about to be born. Replacing his thick lenses for dark glasses, he now considered that he looked the part.

Since it was Saturday night, Queenie's Castle was crowded with young people. They drank a lot and danced wildly and watched the nude floor show with great enthusiasm. Queenie was perched high on her stool with a vacant expression on her face.

'What's up with the Queen tonight?' asked one of the smartly dressed part-time ladies who ran the weekend bar.

'She looks sloshed,' whispered back her companion. 'Never seen her drunk before. Usually all that gin she puts away each night seems to have no effect upon her.'

'Yes it does,' the other one said. 'She goes icy cold just like she's dead.'

'Oh shut-up, you give me the shivers,' her friend snapped back.

Queenie shot them a cold glance as she caught them gossiping. Indeed, in that mask-like face, only the deep-set eyes seemed alive.

At nine o'clock the crew of the ship at anchor arrived in the public bar just for a quick drink before they sailed. This unofficial shore leave had gone on for years, and the local residents were quite used to these seamen. Usually they all mixed well together but tonight the sailors kept to themselves and did not mingle. A tall man who was holding a bag drank with his compatriots and then left, but he returned later wearing dark glasses and began to get quietly drunk. This was not unnoticed.

'Has that sailor gorn blind or is he just blind drunk?' asked someone with that typical cockney humour. At that moment outside, a taxi stopped by the street corner. Queenie left her stool and went to look out of the front door. She watched silently as a tall man sprang into the taxi. She then returned to her throne casting sullen looks at the staff. Then she began to drink heavily and became quite irritable. But everyone agreed that she was looking spectacular that night, as though dressed for the final curtain, in a low-cut white dress, and diamonds sparkling everywhere, even in her hair. She looked like a fairy princess.

The Polish crew had now left the public bar, carrying off with them their tall associate who seemed to be very drunk. Minutes before time, Queenie angrily clanged the ship's bell and the customers began to leave. Queenie took a sip of gin and stuffed four or five pills into her mouth just as Superintendent Mackenzie came marching determinedly towards her with two plain-clothes detectives and several uniformed constables who barred the entrance.

For the first time that evening, Queenie found her sweet charm. She smiled gently at the policemen. 'Hello, Mac,' she said in her soft voice. 'Brought the whole damn copper station with you this time, have you?' There was a tiny sarcastic edge to her voice as she finished speaking.

'I want no more nonsense, Queenie,' said Mackenzie sternly. 'You've been harbouring a murderer. Where is he?'

'You go and find him,' replied Queenie somewhat sleepily. As she tried to put more pills in her mouth, Mackenzie caught hold of the white bejewelled arm.

'Now, come on, Queenie, cough! Do you want me to take you back with me?'

Queenie's pink tongue came out and suggestively licked those red lips. 'How about a nice farewell drink, Mac?' she murmured.

'Queenie,' Mackenzie shouted. 'We've played silly buggers for long enough. Where is that bloody barman – Joe, whatever his name is?'

By now, the constables were running all over the house, searching for Joe.

'You realise, do you, that you are an accessory to murder?' Mac informed her.

The blonde head nodded and the sweet smile appeared again. 'I did it,' she said quietly.

'All right, love,' replied Mackenzie. 'We have a

good idea who did it. If you help me get him, I'll look after you,' he said.

Queenie put her arms about his neck. 'It's too late, Mac,' she whispered, and passed out.

'She's drunk,' said Mackenzie huskily as he carried her to a seat. 'Found Walowski yet?' he demanded of his men. But the answer was in the negative.

Terry Long bent down and picked up a little glass bottle from the red carpet. Sniffing at it, he went over and lifted the eyelids of the unconscious Queenie. 'We'd better call an ambulance,' he said. 'She's chock full of junk.'

As Queenie was carried out on a stretcher, Mackenzie began to prowl about the house. Upstairs, Joe's rooms were searched very thoroughly, but all they could find was a tape recorder in the sink cupboard.

'Switch it on,' said Mackenzie, and he settled down to listen to the gruff voice of Knuckles O'Leary spilling the beans about the Maisie murder.

'Well, I'm blowed!' exclaimed Mackenzie, when the tape had finished running. 'That bloke was innocent of that kid's murder and he done time for it. I wonder why he popped off O'Leary, then. It seems that there's more to this than meets the eye. Bring this tape down to the station, and arrest that boozy old boy in the cellar. Then go down the street and get Hustler's Pop. He hangs about the corner all day.'

Beery Bill and Hustler's Pop admitted nothing. They'd never heard of Joe Malowski, they said. They were clearly waiting for orders from Queenie but she was still unconscious.

At the hospital, Superintendent Mackenzie sat by her bedside waiting for her to regain consciousness, but she never opened her eyes. A nurse came and put the white sheet over her head. 'It's no good waiting, sir, she's passed on,' the nurse said.

So the Queen had defended her castle to the end, and the secrets of the Ship and Castle were never divulged. The Queen of the East End had fled this world to another castle in the sky.

Chapter Twenty-Five

Love Found

Joe lived as a sailor on that Polish ship for a few months before jumping ship in another European port. Setting up in Paris, he began to make a name for himself as an artist and one day was surprised to see one of his old paintings reproduced in an English newspaper. The caption said that it was the work of an unknown artist whose work was much admired. Joe thought that Marie must have helped to get this recognition for him by taking his pictures to art galleries and dealers. For that he was grateful.

He wrote to John and Marie after that, thanking them for all their help. He also wrote to Anne's parents in Australia, asking them of any news of Anne. He suddenly had a strong urge to make contact with his old love.

Anne's parents wrote back immediately. Their daughter was living and teaching near them in Australia, they told him, and would be very happy to hear from him.

And so it was that one blazing Sunday afternoon, Joe Walowski walked down a dry sandy road in the Australian outback. He approached the little bungalow with a cautious look on his face. He looked much older, the past few years had taken their toll on him. His tall figure was slightly stooped and there was a sadness about his eyes. His clothes hung loosely on his lanky limbs.

In the garden, he could see a familiar shape bending over a flowering shrub. 'Anne,' he called softly. He had written to her and told her exactly when he was coming, so she would not be shocked.

Anne looked up and waved. She walked swiftly over towards him, a warm smile on her pleasant face. Her hair was still blonde, her eyes still clear and sparkling. Her figure was slim, her limbs strong. She had hardly changed at all, Joe thought. If anything, maturity had turned her into a beauty.

Anne reached out to him with both hands. 'Joe,' she said quietly, 'I have been waiting for you. I've been waiting for this moment ever since they came and took you away . . .'

Joe took her hands and pulled her gently against him, pressing her against his body and enclosing her with his arms. He lay his head on top of her smooth hair and shut his eyes. 'Anne, my darling Anne,' he murmured. 'You are the personification of all that's good and pure. I always felt that about you. And now I know for sure.'

Anne smiled and lifted her face up to his, her mouth half-opened to receive his. Tears trickled down her cheeks as he pressed his lips down on hers.

'Now is the time,' he said. 'Now is the time to start life again.'

Anne smiled. 'Yes,' she said. 'You deserve it, and together we can make it good.'

And so where Joe might have spent the rest of his life embittered and ruined by fate, here was an angel who was offering him the chance to put all the horrors of the past behind him. He was a lucky man, and he knew it.